C000196374

THE GOD CHILD

BY THE SAME AUTHOR

THE COMFORTS OF MADNESS (1988)
HOWLING AT THE MOON (1990)
THE ABSOLUTION GAME (1992)
THE STORM-BRINGER (1994)

THE GOD CHILD

PAUL SAYER

BLOOMSBURY

First published 1996

Copyright © 1996 by Paul Sayer

The moral right of the author has been asserted

Bloomsbury Publishing Plc, 2 Soho Square, London W1V 6HB

A CIP catalogue record for this book
is available from the British Library

ISBN 0 7475 2801 2

10 9 8 7 6 5 4 3 2 1

Typeset by Hewer Text Composition Services, Edinburgh
Printed in Great Britain by CLays Ltd, St Ives Plc

Once more, to Anne and Simon

ACKNOWLEDGEMENT

I would like to thank the Society of Authors and the K. Blundell Trust for their kind support during the writing of this book.

P.S.

PART ONE

1

'I hate the wind. The way it bangs off the sea. You think something dreadful's going to happen.' Mother lit a cigarette. She eased herself up on her high stool at the end of the bar, wincing with the effort. 'Did I tell you Lionel thought he saw Maisie the other day?'

'No.'

'Down the end of the prom. He swore it was her.'

I left my place behind the bar to close the curtains on the big bay window. Night was coming, the sky all shades of charcoal, the wind prising last season's litter from its hiding holes, making it fly about the dip from the hotel to the seafront.

Mother tossed a crisp to Kipper, her white Scottie. The dog sat and yapped for more. 'No-o. One's enough. It's junk food, my lovely. Bad for you.'

This exchange, its intimacy in the otherwise empty room, irritated me. I loved my mother, but I wished she would be quiet. There was too much on my mind, rage and reason in sumptuous amounts, vying for dominance. In my pocket was a letter from my estranged wife's lover. *In Greece, at this time of year, the light is particularly fine, Harold. Especially in the late afternoon, with the evening to come and all it might promise . . .*

3

Back behind the bar, I refilled Mother's glass with the red wine she had heard was good for someone like her – the possessor of a new shiny chrome prosthesis where once there had been a rotten hip. She took the glass and tipped back her head, drinking medicinally, in doses. Putting the glass aside, she smoothed out a bar towel, patting its corners. Then she scratched her neck, a victim of the silence, looking round at the unused red vinyl seats, the copper-topped tables, the dried flowers in a lit recess, a poster for a new lager on the door, keening to seduce. Elsewhere about the walls were some of the oils she had painted herself, views of the bay and Oughton Head, copied from postcards. 'Be a love,' she said. 'Put the music on.'

I went into the office that linked the bar with the lobby of the Finlandia, our ten-room, two-houses-knocked-into-one, bits-and-pieces hotel. The moments of isolation liberated another stab of anger. *Nicola wants me to tell you about the way the light makes her skin so golden, the shadow of her breasts on the sheet* . . . My face tingled with indignation.

Through the open door, across the reception desk, beyond the wintering potted palm, the empty wire leaflet stand, I could see my reflection in the glass of the main door. Nicola, my wife, had once remarked on my short, rounded build. She said I looked like a badly made vase. It was a shape associated with manic depressives. There was a name for it, and she would look it up some time and tell me. But it had only been her way of getting at me, a projection of one of her own sulky moods. The letter would have been prompted by her, at a point beyond the slow burn of her sullenness, on the cusp of some frothing anger. And by now, such was her way, she was probably regretting it, chewing

Panadol, her big eyes heavy with guilt, though in her head a blank nothing. I was thinking this, trying to believe it, as I fiddled with the buttons of the grimy old tape deck on the shelf. I returned to the bar.

Mother was picking her nails. 'Will you go round some time, Harold? See if she's there?'

'Who?'

'Maisie, silly. Haven't you been listening?'

'Sorry, yes. I'll go in the morning.'

The music came on, the Mighty Wurlitzer pounding out 'The Theme from Van Der Valk'. It made the emptiness of the room emphatic.

The letter crinkled in my trouser pocket. I was sick with annoyance, holding it with the stiff posture of the hotelier, hands behind the back, white jacket buttoned, a pose my father had enjoyed when he was alive and running the place. And there was something in this stance, its suggestion of humility, that afforded a kind of solace, a dignity in suffering, a means for reflecting on my situation. So I had a broken marriage. So I was a bankrupt. So my wife was taunting me, by proxy. I thought, These things are sent to try us. But the humour I was looking for eluded me. Since my return to the family hotel, three months before, I had felt my self-esteem restoring itself, piece by piece. I had improved so much. And Mother was pleased to have me around, taking over the running of a business that was getting beyond her. It had been a time of healing, until the postman came that morning, hitching up his red and blue bag, handing me the letter across the desk with a wink and a twitch as if he knew its contents.

'Are you going out tonight?' Mother's words were slow and careful, delivered in the classless accent she reserved for the guests, the old Yorkshire clippedness smoothed

5

away over years of standing aloof from those who gave her a living.

'Yes, I think so. Friday night. It's become a bit of a habit.'

Mother lit another cigarette as if needing it to cope with this modest news. Her shaking white fingers reached for the ashtray. The Mighty Wurlitzer's electronic backbeat pinged from 'Van Der Valk' to 'I Should Be So Lucky'.

'Lionel will be here at seven,' I said, looking to reassure her. 'Not that there's much for him to do.'

She glanced at herself in the mirror tiles under the spirits shelf, fluffing up her white permed curls. 'He'll tell you he saw Maisie. He's sure it was her.' She drew on the cigarette, elbows on the bar like a hardened drinker.

'I thought she wasn't due back till Easter?'

'So did I.'

'Have you rung the house?'

'This afternoon. There was no answer. But it was a funny ring, like there was someone there refusing to pick the thing up.' She finished her drink, her worn teeth magnified by the glass.

I said, 'Maybe he's made a mistake.'

'I hope so. I hope she's not in any trouble.'

It was nearly seven o'clock. I leaned against the door-frame and loosened my tight jacket, ready to go the moment Lionel showed. Then voices sounded in the lobby and an elderly couple, the Millyons, came into the bar. Mother put out her cigarette and sat up straight. The Millyons came to Oughton Bay every March and they currently represented half the Finlandia's clientele. Their appearance had brightened Mother more than usual this year since Mrs Millyon was also the owner of a false hip and there was much talk of it between them, my mother ever keen to solicit the other woman's seasoned reflections on the condition. They talked happily while I fixed drinks for Mr Millyon.

At five past seven the front door opened and closed, a gust of cold air filtering all the way through to the bar. Lionel came in rubbing his big hands. 'Evenin', Harold.' He smiled at Mother. 'Hello, Peggy. Bit wild out there.' He went into the office to hang his coat and returned, fastening the buttons of his own white jacket.

'I was telling Harold about Maisie,' said Mother.

'Yeah. Right. Well, I'm damned sure it was her, you know, the hair and that. Though I got the feeling she didn't want to see me. Turned right round, she did. Can't think why.' He was looking at me, one eyebrow raised, perhaps hopeful of the scent of some family rift.

Lionel was about thirty-seven, two years younger than me, yet with his rough and ready manner I always felt him to be older. He was an ex-soldier with stiff auburn hair and the grazed complexion of a native of the coast. His father and mine had been great friends, and Lionel had worked at the Finlandia since he left the army. But he did not like me, resenting my abrupt reappearance, feeling I had usurped his position as second fiddle to my mother. Maybe he thought I had come back for my inheritance. I had not. The Finlandia's only real value was in the building itself, and there was a constant rolling loan secured on the strength of that. Besides, I did not think like that anyway, though Lionel would never have believed me. I handed him the hotel keys, finding it difficult to look at him.

'I'm going out,' I said. 'Will you be all right?'

He grinned. 'Always have been, Harold. I think we can cope, don't you, Peg?' He winked at Mother and made a show of checking the bottle shelves.

7

'Good. Well, I'll be away then.' I waved to Mr Millyon who was sitting alone across the room, and went for my coat.

Two minutes later I was walking through what passed for Oughton Bay town centre. On Ash Street the shops were all closed, save for the off-licence with its odd customers and their bulging carrier bags. Along the pavement the last of the hardy day-trippers were heading for their cars, oxygenated and tired from risking their hearts in clambering along the Head. And the wind's slapping hands were at my back, the Mighty Wurlitzer still pinging in my head, stuck between chord changes. *It's an hour since I had her, Harold. Soon we'll be doing it again. Do you know how it feels to make someone satisfied? Nicola says you don't. That amazes me! She's such a great fuck* ... The rage rushed again, a hot poison in the veins. But what could I do? This had to stop. Change your thoughts, switch off the machine, hold the breath. It seemed to work. I hated the world for seven more paces on the resort's damp streets, then I hated no one, the anger melting into a more heartening sense of injustice. The letter was still in my pocket. What was I keeping it for? Evidence? The divorce would be a straightforward matter, with nothing but a few possessions and the last of our debts to argue about. Later I might burn the letter. This idea pleased me, the ritual disposal of an instrument of cruelty I did not deserve. The divorce could be through within three months, and at some point I might ask Nicola about all this. Or maybe not.

Along Station Rise there was more life to the town. Traffic turned on the roundabout. The lights of the Shell garage were burning red and yellow, flooding the wet road with a haloed pink wash. Further on, a few people were entering the Trawlerman's Arms, my destination that night. The

8

Mighty Wurlitzer had been defeated and my mood was picking up, heading for that equable plain from which I believed I had viewed the world throughout my life. I might have been the right shape, but I was no manic depressive. Indeed, my tread was light and even as I approached the Burnt Offerings chilli house, one of Oughton's more successful new enterprises, and glanced through the window.

I was already past the restaurant when I realised I knew one of the faces inside. I stopped outside the wool shop next door and went back, looking carefully from the side of the steamy glass until I could pick it out again among the diners, that known pretty mouth, the watchful eyes and blonde hair of my niece Maisie.

2

About Maisie, it goes like this.

She is my older brother Matthew's daughter. Twenty years ago Matthew and his wife, also Maisie, are heading out of Glasgow. They have been to an end-of-term party at the college where my brother teaches building techniques, bricklaying, roofing, the like. He is the worse for wear, dozing on the back seat while Maisie senior does the driving. As yet, Maisie the child is not with us. She is the New Year's big event, two months from her scheduled appearance.

At a snowy, quiet junction there's a scream. A lorry carrying steel pipes, its driver lost, trundles from the gloom. Its weight crushes the car like a cellophane packet. The scream is halted. An hour later, a doctor is leaning over Matthew telling him they may be able to save the baby, but not his wife.

For five weeks Maisie senior is kept on a life-support machine, my brother with his broken arm and nose keeping vigil on her unmoving face, on the tubes and the monitor which show the foetus's thumb-sucking profile. Then they think it is safe, as safe as possible, and they perform their Caesarean ritual. Seraphic whispers, the descending divine hand from the Scottish sky, and the child is delivered. A miracle baby, salvaged on the whim of a God none of us really believes in, save my father who claims religion as one of his token eccentricities. He weeps at the wonder of it all, calling the infant the God Child. But the holy benevolence does not extend to Matthew's wife. The baby is held to her quiet dry breast and, a day after the birth, the machine is switched off.

Matthew, scarred with remorse, brought Maisie up on his own in a house across Oughton, the place he moved back to when he, like me, felt beaten by the world and needed his family around him. Now Maisie was nineteen and studying English at Newcastle University. Matthew was in Kuwait, teaching on a lucrative two-year contract, catching up on some of the life he had missed. Quite right, I told him. He left in mid-December, just after I had turned up at the hotel. Watch out for Maisie, he said. Be a mate. He scratched his moustache, picked up his big old suitcase, left. And suddenly I was central to my family's needs, after years of being away.

I kept my watch from the side of the window. Maisie was sitting on a bench seat at a table one row forward from the counter. The hair was fashionably straggly, thicker than when I had last seen her in the New Year. She was wearing a scuffed leather jacket and a long denim dress. Opposite her was a young man, about twenty, with a long jawbone, small eyes and a short brown fringe. He was concentrating on the meal, jabbing with the fork, chewing determinedly and talking at the same time as if trying to convince Maisie that the food was good. But my niece's head was on one side, the skin winter pale.

Looking at her for those few seconds stirred my sense of family loyalty. I felt responsible for her, a wholesome sensation for someone who has lived most of his life to suit himself. It banished completely my disaffections about

Nicola and the letter. I thought about knocking on the window, but I did not want to interfere. Maisie was a young woman now, with the wisdom and wariness of an only child. Her uncle would call on her in the morning and we would have a good-humoured, adult chat. I turned away to the end of the parade of shops, over the level crossing and into the Trawlerman's.

In the lounge was Colin, one of the few surviving acquaintances of my Oughton youth. In a way, he was a test of my feelings about the town. He had stayed here while so many of us had drifted inland or abroad. His business was chiropody and he had ploddingly built up his practice in the town and the villages round about. Mother was one of his clients. She liked Colin, his watery humour, the shambling slip-on-shoed walk and rheumy eyes. Once she said he had a personality like Germolene.

He nodded and I went to the bar and bought pints for us both.

'Bloody windy, Harold.'

'I'd noticed.'

'Been busy?'

'Far from it.'

'I know what you mean. I suppose we're all in the same boat this time of year.'

'Things will pick up.'

He reached for the fresh glass, frowning. 'Will they?'

At school, Colin and I had never really known each other. I remembered him as a loner, difficult, a mother's boy who wore thick-ribbed, home-knitted jumpers even in the middle of summer. He would do passable impressions of Deputy Dawg and Spook from *Top Cat*, yet he had no real friends. When he was ten he got into trouble, mistakenly, for the breaking of a cold frame in a garden next to the school.

12

I could still picture him standing in front of the class, agonising wretchedly over where his loyalties should lie. Everyone expected him to single out the real culprit. But it went the wrong way. He could neither accept the blame nor point out the true villain, and he stood bawling his eyes out till the teacher sent him to the headmaster for a beating. He never mentioned it afterwards, but it was a black few minutes he probably remembered to this day. And maybe it was because I was the one who had hoofed the ball over the wall that even now I felt the need to afford him a certain charity.

The room was half-full, all ages, though the young were the loudest, restless-limbed and demanding, with a tribal eye for each other. No doubt they were considering the weekend ahead and the indulgences they might seek, despite the fact that most of them would be out of work until the season got under way.

Colin was watching them. 'You wonder where they get the money,' he said.

'Yes.'

A group of five young people were standing by the jukebox, the two girls keeping close to each other, the boys with their gelled hair and glistening cheeks competing to see who could make the girls laugh the most. The smallest youth went to the bar to demand that the music be turned up. He'd paid his quid, hadn't he? The landlord, a bald fat man in a white shirt, wearily complied. Colin tutted, but I did not mind. I used to like rock music, though my appreciation required a concentration I could not muster these days. And I had been made sceptical by the years. Popular culture could not be sold to me any more.

Now we could barely hear each other speak. I drank my beer and looked up at the lobster pots and blue nylon fishing nets suspended from the ceiling, wondering where they got them from since there had been no commercial fishing in Oughton for sixty years. The town's salvation was its tug at the visiting hearts full of childhood holiday memories, and its geography, the Head and the clean safe sands sweeping south. Otherwise Oughton was a time warp where the shops still closed on Wednesday afternoons, where the locals bad-mouthed their ways through the winter, a place bereft of real industry, floating in the air with nothing beneath to catch it should it fall. In our two tumultuous years of marriage, I brought Nicola here just once, thinking she might be charmed by the sweep of the bay, enlivened by the crisp autumn air. But it rained the whole weekend and she sulked the time away feigning a cold. Small towns did not suit her. They were, simply, not big enough for her.

Colin went to the bar to complain about the noise, something he always took personally. There was no real need for it, I thought. The kids were enjoying themselves, harming no one. I often felt I might have made a decent father, sympathetic towards the needs of the young. But Nicola had not been able to have children. Maybe if she could have got pregnant, with a different set of hormones? Maybe, maybe . . . Fuck it. It would not happen now, for either of us. Maisie was as close as I would get to having someone of my own, and perhaps that was enough.

Colin returned, pleased by getting the music reduced a decibel or two. 'They don't know what peace and quiet is.' And he entered into a tiresome appraisal of the way he dealt with his own two children's noisy excesses.

The crowd was building up in front of us, reaching our table. I thought of the emptiness of the Finlandia. Colin would undoubtedly prefer it there, though I would not encourage the idea. I needed this, needed to be out and away from Mother. I listened to him, nodding mechanically, his talk making me vaguely impatient. 'You see, Harold, there's no discipline, no respect any more . . .' Who did he drink with before me? Perhaps no one. The lonely child now a lonely man. I was drinking steadily, watching the people around me, when the door opened and the young man I had seen in the Burnt Offerings came in, Maisie trailing behind him. Colin saw them too.

3

'Isn't that Matthew's girl?'

'Yes. Maisie.'

Colin's look changed to a stare. 'I thought she was at university?'

'She is.'

This was none of his business. With no explanation, I stood and went sidling through the crowd to my niece.

'Maisie?'

'Oh, Harold. Hi.' She rarely called me uncle now, though the use of my name on its own still sounded self-conscious.

I smiled. 'You should have told us you were here.'

She shrugged, still a girl, caught out playing hookey. Her skin was as unblemished as ever, though there was a line at each side of her mouth that I had not noticed before. And she seemed a little taller with even more of Matthew's willowiness – a family trait that had not been passed on to his younger brother. But her lips were anaemic, giving the impression of a tired adult, overworked and half asleep behind the greying blue eyes.

'Do you want a drink?' I asked.

'Guy's getting them.'

'Let me. Let me treat you.'

16

'No. It's OK.'

The young man, Guy, was deep in the huddle at the bar, waving a ten-pound note to get the attention of the staff, a gesture I always found irritating. 'Boyfriend?'

She wrinkled her nose. 'No. I know him, that's all.'

I made a point of inspecting Guy, at least what I could see of him, the elongated profile of his face, the back of his head, boyishly flat. He was wearing a mauve sweatshirt with the logo DO IT! in yellow reflective letters on the back. He looked small among the men around him, underage. 'Can't say I've seen him before. Is he local?'

'No.'

It was reasonable to assume they were staying at Matthew's place together. The idea warmed me, and I felt a new and larger sense of myself as a brotherly presence in her life, keen to share the secret and to keep it from Mother. Guy came back carrying a bottle of the expensive Mexican lager that was currently fashionable among the young. From his tiny hips I could see he was slim, almost wasted.

'This is my uncle,' said Maisie. 'Harold.'

Guy took a swig from the bottle and nodded. 'How're you doin', Harold?' The accent was standard Geordie, the attitude youthfully dismissive. He took hold of Maisie's elbow.

'Actually, I wouldn't mind staying here,' she said. 'It's been ages since I saw my family.'

Guy looked at me, a flash of contempt in the small eyes. 'We're over here.' He pointed at a small empty table in a corner, beyond the entrance porch that divided the room in half. 'Be seein' you, Harold.' He pushed between us, showing me the boy's shoulders beneath the overshirt, the words DO IT! presented to my face. The rudeness made me bristle.

'Hang on a minute . . .' But he was already pulling Maisie away. I stood my ground for a few seconds, watching as they sat down, Maisie looking serious, avoiding my stare. Then I went back to Colin, thinking I would keep my eye on the door and engage them both if they decided to leave.

'He looks a charmer,' Colin said, sweeping back his hair.

'Yes. Isn't he just.'

Colin went to the bar.

My heart was fluttering from the young man's bad manners. It made me feel weak and inept, lamely considering the various approaches I might take with this Guy. Or maybe it was nothing? He was young and rudeness, after all, was a prerogative of youth.

A minute later, before Colin returned, a disturbance broke out across the room, a progressive pub tumult known only too well by me – the rumble of furniture on wooden floors, breaking glass, a woman's cry, and an abrupt silence among those who could see what was going on. My heart gave again, as it did at any hint of aggression. The talk around me resumed in cool tones, but Colin was looking my way, nodding me across.

A dozen or so people had gathered around the incident, the focus of their attention being Guy, who was standing by a fallen chair, furiously wiping drink from his jeans. Maisie was sitting at the table, head in hands. Behind me, the landlord was making his way from behind the bar, his face clotted with contempt. I tried to shove through the bodies in front of me, but their company hardened, pushing back to make a gangway for Guy, who had dragged Maisie to her feet and was pulling her towards the door. 'Maisie!' But she hurried tearfully along behind this loathsome young man.

I went after them without a thought, catching them in the street and grabbing Guy's shoulder from behind. 'What's the game, eh?' He lurched round, ready to hit me, but I had him at arm's length, ready to duck if he swung his fist. He kept his hands down. I could smell the lager on his breath. He wriggled free of my grip.

'Fuck off, fella. This is nothin' to do with you.' He turned to Maisie, glaring, trying to dismiss me as some minor irritation.

'I think it is,' I said, though my arms had gone limp.

He turned on me, scowling, pushing out and launching me back two paces. 'I said shove off, didn't I?' The action was a pure affront. It brought a bravery to life in me, this confrontation heading instantly for the basest of conclusions. I would probably come off the worst, but I wanted to hit him, or at least land the first blow. I took a step forward. Maisie came between us.

'It's all right, Harold.' Her hands rose and fell loosely at her side. 'I'm OK. Really.'

'It doesn't look that way to me.'

Guy made a move around her, jabbing his finger at me. 'This is none of your business. Right?'

'Leave him alone!' Maisie yelled. 'Oh, come on. Let's bloody go.'

He gave me a primitive look, the glare of a street rioter. Then he put his arm around Maisie's shoulders, drawing her away.

'Maisie?'

She looked back, her hair down over her eyes. 'I'll call you. I'll come and see you tomorrow.'

'No. Wait!' But they were running across the busy road, Guy holding her arm, dodging between the passing cars.

I watched them disappear over the railway crossing and

down a street of semi-detached houses. After a few deep breaths of the cold night air I went back inside the pub, sweating, attracting a few sidelong looks from the people nearest the door. Otherwise, the Friday-night rowdiness had been restored to somewhere near its usual peak.

'Who the bloody hell's he?' Colin was smiling, eyes wide and clear. He was enjoying all this.

'I don't know. Some lout.'

An hour later, we both went home.

The agreeable mild drunkenness I sought on evenings like this had not been achieved. I felt a rustling disaffection with all of my life, with the culture of bars and beer and brewery signs among which I had spent most of my adult days. It was a dreary society, gutter life. And then there had been the letter that morning. It was a low point, and the adrenaline that the incident with Guy had released would not dissipate. I was gloomy and angry, and if he were to reappear again that night, I would be ready for him. My pace quickened. I was ready to take on the world, an alertness in my arms, a readiness, even a wish, for trouble of any kind. Yet, in my heart, I knew that by the next day I would regret this pointless, reptilian state of mind.

I took the longer route home, down the ravine road to the deserted seafront. The wind had dropped to a chafing cold breeze, the tide rolling in, its lapping mingled with the strains of a nightclub disco somewhere up the north side. I slowed to a stroll along the promenade, past the newly painted white railings, the lifebelts in their red boxes, the closed-down lifeboat shop, a dismantled play area and the drained boating pool. I stopped to look at the orange half-moon and its columnar reflection on the sea. It was not soothing. I had seen it too often. I carried on to the winding avenue that led up from the southern end of the promenade, through Oughton Bay town, still in its winter sleep, waiting for the sun and light nights. At the top I walked along the crescent of white-fronted Georgian houses that led to the Finlandia.

Mother, reliably, had gone up to the family rooms at the top of the building. The soft white glow at her bedroom window meant she was either reading or had fallen asleep, leaving the light on as some vain defence against the wind. In the lobby I found Lionel sitting behind the desk, reading the evening paper. He had taken it on himself to close the bar early. I made no mention of it and sent him home. After checking that the Millyons and our other guests, a young, well-spoken couple called Holding, were in their rooms, I sat in the office and poured a hefty scotch from the bottle I kept in the desk drawer. I smelled it and drank, putting my tired feet up on the little safe on the floor by the desk. Now, at last, I might find the intoxication I was after. Sleep would be a blessing since, in all respects, this would be a day to forget.

It was almost twelve and I was feeling better, catching a stray intuition of the Harold I believed in, a man of calm and humour, of smartly pressed shirts and quiet intelligence. I poured a second drink and set it down ready for when I had locked up and put on the night light behind the reception desk. I had picked up the keys and was on my way to the kitchen to check the back door when the phone rang in the office.

'The Finlandia.'

'Harold?' It was Maisie.

'What's the matter?' There was a warmth in my voice. My niece would be witness to my rediscovered self.

'Oh, God, you've got to come. Please. Please, now!' She sounded hysterical.

'I don't know what you're talking about. What do you mean?' I gave a little chuckle.

'I can't believe it. I can't, I can't . . .' Her voice was rushing. She was gulping air.

'Maisie?'

'Oh, Harold, Harold . . .'

I sat down. 'Maisie, calm down. Is it that man?' There was no answer. I felt my dislike of Guy returning in a more mature form, solid and sobering. 'Maisie, has he hurt you?' She began sobbing, a low wail. I thought she might hang up. 'Maisie? Tell me what's the matter.'

'Harold, he's dead. Oh, God!'

'Don't be silly.'

'I mean it, oh, dear Jesus!'

'What do you mean, he's dead? Has there been an accident? Maisie?'

'No, no . . .'

'Then what? Tell me.'

The weeping became hard and guttural, interspersed with a shrill, wet cry: 'I've killed him. He's dead, he's dead, he's dead. Jesus, help me . . .'

4

A car passed in the street, the aura of its lights sweeping past the hotel door. The line went quiet, Maisie's hand over the mouthpiece. 'Maisie?' She removed her hand. Her breath was fast and light, like a lover's. 'Maisie, are you all right?'

'No, I'm not. I don't know what to do. Uncle Harold?'

'Yes, yes. I'm still here.'

'Please help me, please help me . . .' The breath grew more rapid, whiny.

'Maisie, I will. Look, slow down. Tell me, very carefully, what's been going on.'

'I can't. Oh, God, what're you waiting for? I've told you what's happened!' The sobbing began again.

I sat back, looking down at the scratched grain of the desk, the worn green carpet beneath my feet. I could not think. The barrage of weeping was real enough, but I could only believe she had made some kind of a mistake, an adolescent misjudgement. Maisie was being silly. 'Listen – '

'Jesus, what a mess.' Her voice was deep, more composed. 'I might as well kill myself. It's the only way out. I can't go on after this.' It was as if she was addressing herself.

Her words woke me up. The impulsiveness of youth,

seeking drastic solutions to the smallest of problems. She might really do something stupid just to be believed. 'Hey, hang on a minute!'

'It's a nightmare. But God, that's just it. If only it was that. If only I could wake up . . .' Now it sounded like rambling, a wakening mania.

'Maisie, listen. I'll come round. I'll be there in five minutes.'

'Oh, shit, shit! He's dead, he's dead . . .'

'Maisie, just pull yourself together. Stay calm and wait for me. Promise? Maisie?'

A slurred word, a swallow. 'Be quick, Harold. Please, be quick?'

'I will. Don't worry. Five minutes and I'll be there.'

She put down the phone.

Once again, in the stillness of the hotel, I told myself it would be nothing, the stuff of melodrama, like one of Nicola's tantrums. It would be down to inexperience, and I felt for the way Maisie had revealed her immaturity. She'd killed him? He would be drunk, doped, seeking attention in some bizarre, childish way. Now I felt angry with Maisie, dragging me out at this time of night. I was too old for this kind of nonsense. I left the office to lock the main door and came back for the keys to Mother's old Volvo. I drank the whisky, went through the shadows of the kitchen and out of the back door to the garage that stood alone in the corner of the hotel's garden.

The light went out in Mother's room. She was awake and certain to hear me. Yet what was the point in creeping about? There was nothing the matter. Still, when I had eased out the car, I got out and closed the garage doors. If I was gone some time, at least she wouldn't be able to tell if the car was there or not. My discretion was something Maisie might appreciate when this foolishness was over.

The drive across the town took only a few minutes. The booze I had gone through would take me twice over the limit, but the risks here were small and I need only drive normally to avoid the attentions of any late-night police patrol. My head felt very clear anyway. I was rational, an adult about his grown-up business, the peacemaker in some daft tiff between my niece and her boyfriend. And that was how I saw my role. I would be articulate, sternly direct. I would send Guy packing.

The cottage where Maisie and Matthew lived was at the southern end of town on the last stretch of road before the clifftop golf course. There were lights on in the lounge and front bedroom. One of the houses next door was empty and had been up for sale for years. The other was a weekend retreat, but there was no car outside and it was darkened with the downstairs curtains open. Beyond this, at the end of the row, was the home of two old sisters, the Charltons, who had lived there all their lives. This too was in darkness. I pulled up outside my brother's house, got out of the car and knocked gently on the door. Maisie's shadow moved behind the orange curtains. It seemed a full minute before she opened the door.

She looked as grim as she had sounded, her nose raw, a scrape of hair over her bloodshot eyes. She shook her drooping head and I followed her into the lounge. The electric fire was on and there were clothes and shoes scattered around, but otherwise there was nothing out of the ordinary.

'Has he gone?' I was keen to get this over with. By now the lad might have come round and disappeared into the night. It would be easier for me that way, though I was stiff with indignation, wanting to confront him about his vile behaviour. It was a point I wanted to make. But Maisie said nothing, falling heavily into my arms, sobbing. 'Hey, hey. Easy now.'

'Harold, I've done it. I've done the worst thing . . .'

I waited until the crying had stopped, holding her head against my shoulder, looking around the room for any other signs of disturbance. She sniffed and raised her head, biting her bottom lip. 'You're going to have to get the police. I can't do it.'

'What do you mean, get the police?' My tone was almost sarcastic. 'Maisie, you keep telling me these things and I don't know what you're talking about. Where is he? Where's Guy?'

She took a deep breath and held it, the effort forcing her upright. She put her hands in a steeple around her nose and screwed her eyes tight, breathing out slowly into her palms. I thought she was on the brink of a fresh bout of crying, but she looked through with all that, drained by it. She waved feebly at the kitchen door. 'In there.'

I nodded knowingly. I was her Uncle Harold, reliable and worldly-wise, used to dealing with life's awkward little problems. *Watch out for her* . . . I would let no one down.

I took the few steps to the door, my feet silent on the carpet, the strong male bringing his wisdom to bear on an overblown trifle. Afterwards I would be lenient with my niece, forgiving. I might even take her for a meal. This incident, if that was what it was, should be no more than a rite of passage for her. In a day, an hour, it would be forgotten. And I would be honourably discreet, I was thinking as I pushed open the door and saw the trainer-clad feet sticking out from behind the kitchen table.

This was where he lay in his drunkenness, bringing an evil to the innocent home of my brother and his daughter. The anger made my forehead hot. I would pick him up, shake him awake and throw him out. He was not to bring his hooligan ways here. He would have to grow up. Then I saw that I would say none of these things.

He was sitting propped between the sink cupboard and the pantry door, his expression one of total forgetfulness. He did not look anything like the youth I remembered from a few hours before. The hot-bloodedness was gone, replaced by a disarming stillness. His eyes were staring into his lap, mouth open in a slit smile that showed the lower part of his top teeth. One hand was on his leg, the other crooked and open at his side. On the sweatshirt was a big dark stain like a continent on a map. A further spill seemed to come from beneath the shirt and onto his jeans, showing red on the buckle of his belt and in the cracks of his palm.

In the fantastic silence I went over and touched the bone of his shoulder. He did not move. I put my hand against his mouth, but there was no breath. I lifted his bloodied wrist with the intention of looking for a pulse, but as I felt its uncanny dead weight, the clamminess of the skin, an ancient wisdom told me there was no point in looking any further. I stood back, the hairs rising on my arms, a trickle of sweat down my spine. And the grievances I had felt against this youth came to a stunning halt. I had not really known him. I never would.

5

All I could do was stare. The proximity seemed to be inviting me to say something. My mouth was open. Nothing came out but my fast, shallow breath. The fact of the situation was too big to accept, yet it was a stilling, inescapable truth, crammed into the small spaces of the kitchen. I licked a droplet of spit from my lip, looking to the side, at the white enamel sink top, the old cooker, the blind-covered window that overlooked the yard. There was a smell of cooking fat and there were pots in the sink. On the draining board were dried scraps of carrot and mushroom, a pan scourer, domestic clutter that made the scene even more surreal, maddening. I backed away to the lounge door, but could not resist a last glance at Guy to make sure it was true, hoping at the last moment for some missed sign that he might still be alive. But there had been no mistake.

In the lounge, Maisie was sitting on the edge of the armchair by the fire. She could not look at me, and I had no comfort for her. She was already a possessor of this awful knowledge. Used to it. 'Will you ring them?' A calm statement, the voice of someone older. The Maisie I thought I knew was a mythical figure, an invention of family sentiment.

I closed my eyes, feeling faint, the shock almost tangible. 'What?'

'The bloody police. Who else?'

I sat down on the sofa, concentrating on breathing in through my nose and out of my mouth. My involvement was needed, but I was weak and nauseous. After a minute or so, the faintness passed. I felt the pull of the easy way out, the obvious – ring the police and hang around here till they came and took away my niece, this woman who had concealed her real self from me all her life. It would be a simple matter. The right thing to do. And over in minutes. My palms were moist. I dried them on my trousers.

'Well?' Maisie said.

'No.' The use of my voice brought back the nausea. I swallowed, trying to think consciously, to restore a sense of time. 'I'm not ringing them. Not till I know what's happened.'

She sighed. 'There's no point waiting. It'll make things look worse.'

'No. No.' The nausea disappeared, yet I was still breathless. I rubbed my eyes, pursuing my elusive adultness, trying to let these grossly misshapen moments pass and get the thing in some perspective. I looked at Maisie. 'It's . . . Just let's think about it a minute.'

'What for?'

'Maisie!' I was angry. I put my hands together, gripping tight. 'Look, these things are never as simple as they seem.' A platitude, a line from a dozen films or more. 'I need to know what's been going on. How this . . . Just what exactly happened.' The trite sentences were queueing up in my head. The role of counsellor was coming with every word I spoke, too readily. I was not up to this.

'What's there to say?'

29

'Plenty, I would think.' It was hard to conceal my impatience, but it brought an awakening of my old self, a click of reason. Maisie was once again the girl I knew, her gaucheness shining from every aspect of her, the trendy hair, the long blue dress, the way she kept covering her face. Then she looked up at me and smiled. A silly smile showing her perfect white teeth. She was a spoilt brat, a child who had taken something from a shop and could not see why she should have been caught. She did not realise what she had done! I felt like shaking her. I stood in front of her, talking to the top of her head. 'Maisie, that boy in there is dead.'

'I know. You don't have to tell me.'

'Then tell me what's happened!'

The smile disappeared, replaced by a sour, bunched expression, eyes squinting, lips peevishly tight. She put her head in her hands. 'I can't, I can't! Don't shout at me!' She gave a wet sob, her fingers wrapped in the waves of her hair. 'I stabbed him.'

There were tiny black spots on the front of her dress. I looked at her hands, the traces of red in the nails and cuticles. A line of smeared fine dots ran across the back of her wrist and along the inside of her arm. She had tried to rub it off. The effort that must have taken, the horror of this last hour or so, made my annoyance seem thoughtless.

She looked to her side, at the fire and its fake glowing coals. 'They'll lock me up, Harold. I'm fucking done for.'

'You don't know that, yet.' I was calmer, pitying her, but the room was constricting. It was not big enough for our momentous concerns. I needed space for my growing comprehension, and to take charge. Crouching in front of her, I put my arms round her shoulders, drawing her head against my chest. The touch made her sob. 'Come on, we'll go.'

'Go where?'

'To our place. We need to go through this. You'll have to tell me exactly what happened. Another hour or so isn't going to make any difference.'

She lifted her head, sniffling. 'It's no good.'

'It *is* good. Do as I say. Come on, Maisie.'

She took a brave look at the half-open kitchen door. I went over to it, putting my hand round the jamb to turn off the light, pulling the door shut. She looked about to say something, perhaps wanting to resist my suggestion and trust to her own instincts. I went to her. 'Come on.' I took hold of her arm, but she stayed where she was, stiff in my grip. It was an impasse. Then she stood and picked up her coat from beside the chair.

'This can't be right,' she said.

'We don't know what's right yet.'

I turned off the fire and checked about the rest of the room. The movement made my thoughts fluid and, for a bizarre moment, the horror of my discovery escaped me. We might simply have been going out for the night. 'Trust me,' I said, though I was not sure why she should, and I led the way to the door, half expecting that she would not follow.

6

'Can you get me some cigarettes?'

I rummaged through the desk drawer for one of Mother's packets. Unable to find any, I went to the vending machine in the darkened bar. As I tapped the buttons, a returning, matured shock set my heart pounding. The same thing had happened in the car on the way back, a panic attack, the streetlit terraces too vivid, as if I had been cast into the essence of their brickwork and windows, and that which was me, my body, was left airless and disintegrating behind the wheel of the car. Here, it was still an atrocious feeling, but easier to deal with. If I thought I was going to pass out, I could lie down on the floor. I was all right here. This was my home. I leaned against the machine until the pounding slowed. I told myself it was late. This could still be a dream. And that helped, displacing the acuteness of the moment. I went back to the office.

Maisie was sitting beneath the small high window, wiping her nose with a tissue. She took the cigarettes and lit one, blowing the smoke out with a spit. She did not look used to the habit. I breathed in carefully, trying to settle my heart's excesses. There was a low whine in my ears. My stomach roiled and my mouth and lips were dry from the booze I had gone through earlier. I resisted the temptation to take the whisky from the desk.

'Feeling better?'

She grinned sourly. 'How could I?'

On the way back she had said nothing, staring blankly ahead, huffing from time to time as if expressing a vague indignation about her predicament. It had still not sunk in. I would have to think for her, to remind her carefully how much she was trapped in the event. I would help. I was her uncle, her ally.

It was important to get her talking. 'Do you want to tell me about it now?'

She looked down at her shoes, grey suede lace-ups, fashionable, manly. The boundaries of gender were getting closer among the young. Had this awful act of hers been an extreme expression of her wish to be ranked equal with the boys, catastrophic evidence of a bitter philosophy she had kept from her family, learned in these recent formative years? The cheap red earrings seemed to give the lie to this, as did the childish Betty Boop watch face. What life had she been imagining for herself when she bought these things? What were her innocent dreams, and what would happen to them now? She lifted her hand from her lap, then let it fall back.

'There was a row,' she said. 'I stabbed him. I didn't mean to. It was a tap. I just thumped him with the thing.' She sounded flat and defensive. These were the words she had prepared for the police.

'What was it? A knife?' She nodded. I tried to get her to look in my eyes, but her gaze shifted to the side, fixing on the pen tray on the desk. 'We have to get this straight. What was the row about? I mean, Christ, who was this lad? Where's he from? What's he doing here?'

33

She winced, biting her bottom lip. 'He's from up . . .' She began, then dried up, tracing arcs in the ashtray with the cigarette. The tears were close again. I thought that I did not know young people. A woman of my own age would have been easier to deal with.

'Where? Newcastle?'

'Somewhere near. I don't know. Maybe Gateshead or somewhere. I don't really know places up there.'

'All right. How long have you known him?'

'Not long . . .'

Guy was a drifter. He dossed around. Last weekend he and a few mates gatecrashed a party at a house in Newcastle. They were selling drugs – Ecstasy, dope – though most of the students weren't interested. 'They're not like people think they are, or what they used to be,' she said. 'Most of them just want to work and get their degrees and find a decent job.' She had been drinking wine, but someone might have put something in it. Maybe it was Guy. He said he'd taken a shine to her. Fancied her something rotten. And Maisie had slipped into this funny mood. It felt good. She was all friendly and kind, even to people she knew she couldn't stand the sight of. It wasn't right, but she couldn't fight it. That was what made her think the drink had been spiked.

When one of her friends, Becky, said she wanted to leave, Maisie said she would go with her. But Guy trailed them, wittering away, trying it on, one line after another. At Becky's flat, there were a few of the rugby lads from the university. She told them Guy was being a pain and they told him to clear off. He wasn't suited to the idea, and it made him angry, as if he had a chip on his shoulder about his better-off, more articulate peers. But there was nothing he could do, he was way outnumbered. Becky invited

Maisie to stay the night, but Maisie was coming down from whatever it was she had taken. She had a headache. The walk back to the flat she was sharing with two other girls might shift it. And it was only round the corner. Still, she gave it an hour, then slipped out down the fire escape. But Guy was in the alley. 'I didn't like what happened there,' he said. 'Why'd you let them do that? Fancy me, don't you?' Maisie tried to brush him off. She was only ten yards and two flights of stairs from Becky's flat. She had dropped the latch on the door, but she could have knocked. She could have knocked and screamed and woken the whole street if necessary. But you're worried about looking stupid. Then you're too frightened to do anything. It happened so quickly. He had hold of her. He was too strong, too angry for her. She thought she had cried out, but no one heard.

The effort seemed suddenly draining. She stopped. I had to ask the next question. I had to be certain. 'Maisie, do you mean he raped you?'

She cupped her mouth, nodding.

So this was the story, and I believed it, sobered by its logic, angered by what Guy had done to a member of my family. I wanted to comfort her in time-honoured fashion, a cuddle, a kiss, but her youth prevented me for some reason. I shifted on my seat, facing the duty roster above the desk. 'This may sound stupid, but couldn't you have gone to the police?'

'I should have done, I know. I meant to . . .' Her voice was cracked and hoarse. 'There's a student counsellor at the university. I wanted to talk to her first. You're a man, you can't imagine it, something like that.' The wounded woman. Already a man-hater? 'You don't know what to do. All those programmes you see on the telly about the police. You don't know what they'll put you through. Then

35

you get to thinking . . .' She took another cigarette from the packet and lit it, blowing the smoke out with a puff of contempt. 'You get to thinking it was all your own fault anyway.'

In the room above the office Mr Millyon stirred and went to the toilet. We waited until he had gone back to bed. I reached for her tiny wrist and squeezed it. She froze at the touch. It was a clumsy gesture. I took my hand away. 'And you didn't get to see this woman?'

'It was a Sunday. There was no one there.'

'There was no number you could ring?'

'There might have been. I didn't have it in me to find out.'

I took the whisky from the drawer. The need was too compelling. I poured one for Maisie. She coughed with the first sip. I asked her if there was anything else she wanted. She shook her head.

'That next day, I just stayed in bed. I told the girls I had a bad stomach. I couldn't face them.' She tutted. 'I felt filthy. Anyway, when they'd gone out that night, I got up. There was a knock at the door. I ran to lock it, but he just pushed his way in.'

'You mean Guy?'

'Yes. Maybe he'd been hanging around waiting for the others to go. I don't know. He tried being nice at first. He said it was a good party. He said I'd given him the come-on. But I hadn't.' Her voice broke into a squeak, her eyes watering. She looked at me, pleading to be believed. 'It was the drink. I told him so. He was trying to be calm, but his eyes had this really glazed look, like he was high. He said I was to forget all about it. It'd just been a bit of fun. I'd been willing. That's what he wanted me to believe. But I couldn't. I said I knew what had happened. Then he told me he had some suspended sentence hanging over him. I don't know what for. He said he was going to Greece in a couple of weeks to work the beach bars or something. I could forget all about him. Then the front door banged. It was someone in the downstairs flat, but I think he thought the girls had come back. He lost his bottle. He didn't want them to see him. But before he went he said he'd fucking kill me if anything came of it.'

'And you believed him?'

She closed her eyes and shook her head. 'I didn't know what to think. He seemed so wild. An animal. I couldn't face lectures the next day. Or the next. I just went round in a daze, trying to think what was for the best. I thought about the hundreds of women it must have happened to, how they probably just clammed up and said nothing. Being a woman, it's so . . .' She closed her eyes and shook her head. 'I kept thinking about Dad. It would kill him if he knew. I felt so awful. I had to get away. In the end I just packed my bag and came down here. I meant to come and see you. You're so like Dad. I thought you'd understand.'

The comment flattered me. I was glad to accept it. 'You should have tried me.'

'I would have done. I just wanted a day or two at home, to be on my own, to get my nerve up. Then Guy turned up. He got the address from someone he knew at the university. It must have been the same person who told him where the flat was. Guy must have had some lever on whoever it was, drugs or something. I can't think how else he could have found out. He didn't even know my second name.'

'When did he get here?'

'This morning. He was nice as pie, but I could tell he'd lost his grip. I tried to humour him. I told him I wasn't going to say anything to anyone, that I'd quit university and everything. I thought it was what he'd want to hear and maybe he'd just go back and it would be all right. Then we saw you and he got paranoid, really rattled. He thought I knew you'd be in the pub. I tried to explain, but he wouldn't listen.' She swallowed. 'We went back to the house. He said some frightening things . . . He said if he was going to go down for one jump, it might as well be two. He put his hands on me. I shoved him off and ran into the kitchen. I was going to run out the back, but the door was locked. There was this knife on the draining board. I thought he might grab it, so I picked it up first and thumped him with it. I couldn't believe it. It just went straight in. Oh, God!' She leaned on the desk. 'Uncle Harold, what am I going to do?'

The pity rose in my chest. This was such a mess. Her talk lay in my head, a raft of information that would have to be dealt with coolly. I needed to be alone for a while. I picked up my glass and went through the door, standing at the reception desk, looking at the shadows in the lobby, my back to Maisie. The distance seemed necessary. I looked at the fake plaster arches, the block-patterned carpet, that same stretch of floor my father used to tell me off for running across. The conventional thoughts about what might happen to Maisie drifted in and out of my mind, the unsympathetic interrogations of the police, the fact that she might not be able to prove the rape. There would be headlines, Matthew being dragged back from Kuwait. *We could all live without that.* And I knew Maisie. I was certain of her innocence. But she might not be believed. This possibility laid bare the reality of the situation. She was so young. Her life had hardly started. And she was family, of my blood, the miracle baby, for God's sake. I tried to weigh up the value of conscience, how long the guilt over such an incident might last, how genuinely malign it might be, *how one might feel if* . . . And here a new option came flickering to life, something already known, yet dismissed by the conscious mind through a lifetime of trying to live by some unwritten code of honesty. What if she tried to get away with it?

The balance of reason tipped. It was an overwhelming notion. The odds might be very good. Guy was a waster. Maybe no one knew he was here. The idea grew with the slow minutes, taking on a life of its own. Suddenly I was open to no other suggestions. It made my arms limp. It was something I could do. The haunting conscience, the criminal's later life stricken with guilt, was the stuff of soap operas. If I were to attempt this, all I had to do was not think about it.

I turned back to the office door, the idea on my lips. Maisie was shifting on her seat, looking round for something. I turned away again. Maybe the drink was informing my sense of logic? Yet the chances were undoubtedly good. Right was on our side. I grinned nervously, my head racing with this last thought. And time was against us. It called for a decision. It was what *I wanted to do*. I went back to Maisie.

'Who do you think might miss him?'

She was trying the whisky again, screwing her face up at the taste. 'Oh, God, I don't know. His friends maybe.' She put down the glass. 'This is pointless. We've got to get it over with.'

'Maisie, listen to me – '

'I've got to do it. I'll ring the police myself.' She reached across the desk for the phone.

In my growing excitement, the action annoyed me.

Couldn't she see I had all the answers? I pushed the phone away. 'Don't.'

'I have to.'

'Maisie.' I put the phone on the floor, a tiny act in the space of which my decision was made. It was almost a relief to be rid of the terrible uncertainty. I looked at her for any sign of interest in the fact that I was about to instantly relieve her pain. She leaned back in the chair, her hands in her lap. She was exhausted. It would help my cause. 'Maisie . . .' I stood square in front of her. She looked up. It was the expression I wanted, worried and frightened, a look my gambolling plan craved by way of reinforcement.

I put my hands on her shoulders. They were small under the denim of the dress, the bones sharp.

'I'll get rid of him.'

7

'You can't! You can't do a thing like that. It's a dumb idea. It's wrong.'

'What's so wrong about it? What's he done to you?'

Maisie put her hands over her face. 'Harold, no!'

'Honestly, Maisie, it can be done. If we're careful.' I was almost enjoying the possibility of it all, getting high on my decisiveness. Tomorrow I would regret it. But tomorrow was a black demon against my wish for action, my wish to feed on the impulse. I was standing, looking down at the top of Maisie's head. I could be so valuable to her. Why couldn't she see that? 'The majority of things like this are never solved. Did you know that?' It was something I had seen on television within the last week or two, a documentary I had hardly been paying attention to. Now it took on an extraordinary significance. It was meant for me, for this very moment. I remembered the comments about the ones who got caught. They were panickers, bunglers, fuddled by the enormity of their act. And they were the ones who had actually committed the crime, in moments of rage that blinded them to the practical, simple practice of hiding a body. I had done nothing. I could think clearly, I could calculate. My role would be that of an accessory and I could live with that.

Maisie was confused. She made as if to stand, then sank back in the chair. The idea was sinking in, but she could not commit herself. I would have to make up her mind for her.

'I can't let you do that,' she said.

'You can. It could be a lot easier than you think.'

She shook her head. 'But what would you do?'

'I'll be the one to worry about that. You needn't be involved. Come on.' I took her hand.

She sighed, eyes closed. 'It wouldn't be right.'

'Why wouldn't it? You're the innocent party here, Maisie. Trust me.' Now I was besotted by the idea. It was a matter of extreme pride. No one could have resisted my sure-mindedness. Maisie gave an odd curl of the lips, as if she had been told off at school. She shook my hand away and stood.

I led her upstairs to the room next to mine. It had once been her father's bedroom, though now it was only used for occasional visits from friends of my mother. I sat Maisie down and turned on the bedside light. Next I brought a duvet from the landing cupboard. She was to get into bed and wait for me. It was as if she was my patient. In whispers, I told her that if Mother appeared she was to say that she'd been unhappy at Newcastle. Her course was proving difficult and the digs were bad. She had been wondering if she had made the right choice and had come home to think it over. But she hadn't liked being in the house on her own. I had met her in the pub, suggested that she stayed here at the hotel, and had driven over to collect her later. She was not to embellish the story without telling me.

'But I haven't got any things with me.'

'It's not a problem. We can sort it out tomorrow.'

'I still don't think it's right,' she said, yet I felt sure I had won her over. The difference in our ages was now clearly defined. I was the grown-up, in control and full of ideas. She reached for the strap of her dress, then stopped. Her head drooped, lips parched white, her skin so grey I was certain she would sleep the moment she slipped between the sheets. I asked her for the key to the house and she gave it to me. It was a critical gesture. I hugged her, told her I would not be long, and went creeping back along the landing, past Mother's door, down the stairs and into the night.

It was two o'clock. The time had passed incredibly slowly, though now it threatened to shoot by. Alone with the idea of what I was going to do, it became wild and reaching. But as I drove back to the house, my excitement was tempered. This really could be the most profound folly. Yet there simply wasn't time to think about it. I could not allow myself the time. Again I thought there really must have been hundreds of cases like this which had never been solved. I had no criminal record, not even a parking fine. And we were a long way from Newcastle. But how was I to do it? A rolling bolt of possibilities kept coming to mind, though I concentrated on the idea of just getting on with the job. The physical act would provide its own answers. The body was the thing, the evidence. It was a hidable, buriable object and I had to get possession of it while it was still dark. It would make the process irreversible. And then? It was too late to do anything else. For that, I would permit myself time to think. First he would have to be moved.

The wind had dropped and the street was quiet. It was dead old Oughton, a deserted holiday town waiting for the sun to climb and the season to jerk it to its half-life. It was sleeping, unwatching, provided I did not disturb it. I drove round to the alley which ran between the rear of the houses and the shoe-box offices of a removal firm. A single security light was on in the compound, shining on a row of four blue vans along one side. It was strong enough to pick out the backs of the houses, the sash windows, the eaves and doors. They could be seen from hundreds of yards away, but there was nothing I could do about that. I pulled up in the shade of a bush at the other side of the fence, a few yards beyond the gate to Matthew's back yard. I switched off the engine. Anyone living nearby might be used to the sound of vehicles moving around the compound at odd hours, yet I must not be complacent. I opened the car door gently and got out. The air was cold and I could feel it down the front of my jacket and the shirt I had been wearing all day. I still had my tie on. I would take it off in the house. It would have been helpful if the wind had still been up, though at least I had the hush of the sea reaching high tide at the foot of the cliffs beyond the next two streets. I carefully raised the latch of the gate, crossed the yard and let myself in through the kitchen door.

There was a smell like cooked apple, and a warmth I had not expected. I looked back into the yard, imagining half a dozen faces watching me. The door would have to be closed before I turned on the light. In the darkness of the kitchen I could not see him. Then I heard an electronic beep. He was not dead. He had come round and was waiting for me, looking for a terrible revenge. I crossed the six feet to the light switch by the lounge door, thinking I would trip over him, that I would hear him groan, or the scuffling of his feet as he lunged at me in the darkness. I used the doorjamb to guide my hand, found the light and switched it on. I turned my head.

Guy was there. Not pretending. Reliably dead. I was sweating all over my body, a trickle on my thigh, my knees weak. I went over to him, took the beeping watch from his wrist, turned it off and dropped it in my pocket. I stood back, getting my breath, the sweat giving a superficial chill to my skin.

The stillness of the scene imparted an appalling reality. The two of us. No one else. At some point I'd had it in mind to fuel the next stage with moral outrage. This creature had raped my niece. He had tainted all our lives, everything we took to be decent. He was trash. I was to hate him. But my mind was completely blank. It was a job I had to do, a lumpen task in front of me, and I was not sure I could go through with it. I took off my tie and looked him over. The facial skin was creamy white, the jowls and neck a dull brownish purple, as if the blood was collecting there, draining from his head. The eyes were losing their colour, rolling back into their orbits. His jeans were wet with piss, the Mexican lager, source of the sickly smell. And above the apex of the stain on his sweatshirt was a tiny perforation. It was barely a rip, a snag that could easily have been mended. It must have been a flukey hit, between the ribs and straight to a heart valve or a major artery.

My breath was coming more easily. I bent over, looking to get hold of him, to test his weight and overcome my reluctance to handle him. Gripping his jeans, I dragged him forward with one hard tug. His head slid down the pantry door and hit the tiled concrete floor with a sickening thud. I pulled him a few inches more. There was a scraping on the floor. I rolled him on his side. For some reason he had been sitting on the knife, a vegetable knife with a dark wooden handle and a slender three-inch blade. Blood had dripped down his side and collected behind him in a

45

thick line against the skirting board, pink where it met the urine on the floor tiles, but his clothes seemed to have absorbed most of it. Crouching behind him, I put my hands under his shoulders and lifted, testing the weight, which I took to be less than ten stone. I shuffled my arms round his front. His back was lukewarm and moist, the DO IT! logo pressing against my own sweat-damp chest. The legs straightened with an eerie slowness as I pulled him up and felt the back of his head, his hair, against my chin. My arms were quivering with the effort, but there seemed no point in hanging around. This was a one-shot task. None of my efforts would ever have to be repeated. I dragged him across the floor to the coir mat behind the back door. His heels left two pink wavy trails. Needing to rest a few seconds, I put him down on the mat, using the time to take a tea towel and run it under the cold tap. I wiped up as much of the mess on the floor as I could find, diluting it to reduce the staining. The job would have to be done properly tomorrow. I put the towel in a bucket under the sink and went back to Guy.

I switched off the light and opened the back door, pushing it against Guy's outstretched legs. In the light from the compound, anyone watching from a bedroom in any house along the row would be able to see what I was doing. It was a chance I would have to take. The procedure was under way and I could not bear to stop. In the dark of the kitchen I flexed my arms, took a deep breath and put one arm under his shoulders and the other under his knees. With one committed exertion I would carry him out, cradle-fashion, to the car. I gripped tight and lifted him up. It was a moment of macabre intimacy, the familiar shape of a body in my arms, my nose banging against his forehead as I juggled him higher. I pushed the door open wide with my foot and lurched onto the flags of the yard. The centre of gravity was too high, but if I was quick I might get through the open gate to the car in one move. I might even be able to get the boot open without putting him down.

But I had only gone three staggering paces when I heard footsteps in the alley. I dropped down in the shadow of the side wall. Guy was still in my arms, but I was on top of him, my head buried in his armpit.

'What's that, then?' A man's voice. He was by the back yard of the house two doors away. He stopped and belched. A late-night drunk. If he came up to the yard wall, he couldn't help but see us. He came closer, his feet scraping on the cobbles, maybe looking for the right gate to his house. The sweat flowed in my hair and down my forehead. I could smell the fabric of Guy's sweatshirt.

The man stopped six feet from my head. He began retching and threw up, two, three expressions, the sick splattering in the alley. A groan followed, then silence. Easing round, I could see the shadow of his head on the bricks of the house, and the open kitchen door. He mumbled, looking about him, towards the car. He lit a cigarette, grunted something angrily, and staggered back the way he had come.

The fear had a reducing hold on me. I could not go through with this. It was the most stupid mistake of my life. But I had to. I had promised Maisie. I could at least attempt the next stage, even if I was to be caught.

I disentangled myself from Guy and went out into the alley. The pool of vomit was in the angle of the wall and the cobbles, further away than I had thought. A voice came from the street at the other side of the house, a shout, followed by laughter. He was a hundred yards off and moving away I hoped. If not, I might still have time. I opened the hatchback boot of the car, threw the jack and an old blanket on the back seat to make more room, and lifted the parcel shelf. I went back for Guy. Half crouching, I dragged him up, out of the gate, and with the help of my feet and knees managed to bundle him over the bumper and inside. I shoved his feet up so that his knees were tucked in his chest, and thumped his head down to get the parcel shelf back. I closed the boot with a quick stab of elation. I locked the kitchen door, closed the yard gate. I backed the car down the alley and drove along the street, seeing the drunk ahead. He was sitting on the pavement, propped against a low wall. He waved weakly as I passed. Surely, he would be too pissed to remember me?

Five minutes later I was back at the hotel. I put the car in the garage, locked the doors and went inside. The light was still on in the office, the whisky and two glasses on the desk. I took the drink Maisie had left and swallowed it in one. The physical effort I had made in less than forty minutes amazed me. I did not feel tired, and for a few minutes I toyed with the idea of finishing the job that night. But I might not last out. I was thirty-nine and given to muscular twinges after the most modest physical effort. And I needed time to work out the next move. I drank one more measure of whisky, rinsed the glasses in the kitchen, and went upstairs.

In the spare room Maisie was lying in bed in her bra, still awake, staring red-eyed at the bedside lamp. The dress and shoes were bundled together on the floor. She turned slowly to face me. I put my finger to my lips. 'It's all right,' I whispered. She nodded feebly, her chin quivering. It gave me a new sense of strength. Now I was a father consoling his child over a nightmare. I suggested she might turn out the light if she could bear it, and in case Mother came prying. I kissed her forehead, closed the door and went to the bathroom. There were brown blood smears on my jacket and shirt front and lighter traces on my trousers. I made a pad of toilet roll, wet it under the tap and took off my jacket and trousers to dab at the stains. I would have to hide them in my wardrobe until I could get to clean them properly. The shirt would have to be thrown away. I urinated, then picked up my clothes.

A piece of paper crinkled in the trouser pocket. *You just didn't know when you were well off, Harold. It's a pity* . . . I took out the letter, ripped it to pieces and flushed it down the toilet.

8

At dawn the gulls awoke all at once, rousing each other with shrieks that built to a grating chorus, then subsided to single cries as they dispersed about their business.

There was an ache in the side of my chest. I felt the bottom rib, finding a pinprick tenderness like the first intimation of a nasty growth. Beneath this was a hint of the muscle solidifying. I lay looking at the ceiling, trying to rest it. I had dozed on and off for two hours. It should not have been enough, but the tension alone might keep me alert for the rest of the day. Besides, how could I sleep? Everything was still to do, a programme unveiling itself, fanning out from the second I had made the decision to get rid of Guy. For a moment I thought about ending it here and now, giving up. I would talk with Maisie. I would look weak and foolish, a drunk regretting his behaviour the morning after, but it would be the sensible thing to do. Then my thoughts melted into nothing as I got out of bed and went to the bathroom to shave, to get some kind of a routine going. It seemed important. And the original plan reasserted itself of its own accord.

Mother would be suspicious. On Saturday mornings I usually slept in. Andy, our chef, would come in at seven, old Mary arriving an hour later to wait on the breakfast tables, clean the bar and change the linen in the guests' rooms. I would take up the running of the place by two o'clock, seeing to any new arrivals, minding the bar until midnight. The Millyons were leaving today. There were two bookings for that night. And if the weather was fair, Tourist Information might ring with more enquiries. The busier, the better. I went back to my room and dressed in an old thick shirt and jeans. I picked up my money, thirty pounds, all I had in the world, and put it in my pocket with the car keys. It was almost seven.

I pulled the duvet back over the bed and sat down. I tried to think of Maisie in the next room. She was barely out of school, her life in ruins. This was all for her. But I could not convince myself. Some of last night's booze was still in my blood, the options muzzy in front of me, unwanted. I wondered again about getting the police. But I could not, must not let Maisie down. She would already be used to the idea of what I was going to do. It would make me despicable, never to be relied on, never the good old Harold again. It was not to be considered. What I was doing was right. Maisie was innocent. It had been self-defence. And surely every family had some dark secret, a moment of aberration in an otherwise blameless life? I could not ponder the moral question. I had to think immorally, a day spent outside the reference of the law. It would be my one evil act, a task performed without thought and forgotten immediately.

I looked around my room with its wooden bed, the old table where I had stood my first mono record player, listening to Fleetwood Mac, Harry J and the All Stars, while I did my homework. In a wall cupboard there were still some of my old games – a battered Monopoly set, Frustration! – which my mother used to lend to the guests' kids on rainy days. The ceiling sloped on the gable side, and the carpet was faded and curling along the skirting board. It was the same space in which I had fought and argued with my brother. Who had looked out for me when I went up to grammar school. Who had driven the car that killed his wife. Who had suffered enough in life.

The thought of Matthew sharpened my concentration. I wished he was here. It would have been so much easier with two of us. I stood to think what I was actually going to do.

Guy would have to be buried. The bay would not do. The sea always returned its dead to the land. Then I remembered a conversation with Colin when he had said, reflecting on some grisly find down the coast, that the landscape round here was probably littered with corpses. And, according to him, the only way to dispose of a body was to cover it in quicklime. It was a sure thing, melting the lot away. Even the teeth. But what did he know? Had his chiropody training extended to such things? Possibly, though I did not know what quicklime was, except that it was something builders used. I watched the clock constantly. The minutes were passing and all I had thought of was to try and find quicklime somewhere. I would have to be more decisive. There was an old coat of mine in the garage, and boots. And a spade. I would go up the coast, not down it. There was a wood I knew . . . The practical considerations made me more hopeful.

It was a quarter past seven. My limbs were heavy from the exertions of a few hours ago, but they would not stiffen up till later in the day. The little pain stabbed in my rib, though I might be able to disregard that once I got going. I walked about the room to get my muscles moving, opening the curtains to look out at the corner of the building where the bathroom was, the moss-edged roof tiles, the uneven

52

sections of old box guttering. Then I looked down at the greenhouse, the rockery, the garage, and Mother walking by the woolly lawn.

She must have risen early, troubled by her hip or my movements in the night. I had not heard her, nor expected she would be about. She was taking Kipper for his morning runaround. The dog watched her from a few yards away as she kicked earth on his droppings in the flower bed and used her stick to push back the weeds by the cinder track that ran round the back of the hotel. When she moved on, the dog stood wagging his tail, eager to keep the distance between them. Mother called to him. From this height I could not hear her voice. The dog barked and ran off, skipping between the cherry trees on the lawn and on towards the pebble-dashed garage. Mother tapped her slow way towards him, standing at a leaning angle, looking at the garage, then making her way to the line of flags that ran along the window side. I pulled on my jumper, raced out of the room and down the stairs.

Andy was in the kitchen, laying out meat from the freezer, the microwave humming at the end of the long worktop.

'Morning, Harold.'

I smoothed my hair. 'Yes. Good morning.'

He was smiling. 'Coffee?'

'Please.' I was trying to see out of the back window without looking too obvious. The microwave pinged.

'A spot of porridge on the go here, if you want some?'

'No, I don't want anything. I'm not hungry yet.'

'Oh, right. One of those nights, was it?'

'No.'

My touchiness registered with the young man. He stroked his unshaven face and turned away, wiping his hands, clicking on the percolator. For a few helpless moments I watched him take his big cleaver to the mushrooms on his chopping board. Then, casually as I could, I went to the window that overlooked the garden. Mother was at the front of the garage, still looking at it, though the dog was away rummaging in weeds at the side of the drive, peeing against the wall. 'Has Mother had breakfast yet?'

Andy had his back to me, looking along the row of ladles, a big sieve, big scissors on the wall. 'She'll be in for it shortly.'

'Maybe she'll want coffee too.' It was a stupid thing to say. He would know what she wanted better than I. He shrugged. Like Lionel, Andy did not care for being told what to do by the proprietress's son who had turned up here on an apparent whim. I looked back out of the window. Mother was coming this way, frowning. She negotiated the few stone steps up to the door one at a time and came in, Kipper skittering round her ankles and onto the tiled floor.

'Something's troubling the dog.' She took off her coat and hooked it on the peg behind the door. 'I wondered if it was the garage. Maybe something's got in there and died. A rat maybe.' She sat down at the big table in the centre of the kitchen. Kipper came jumping up at me, trying to sniff my fingers.

'Get off, damn thing!'

Mother looked at me cautiously, turning back the cuffs of her cardigan. 'If there's something in the garage, we need to know about it. Before the environmental health do,' she said. 'Will you have a look, Harold?'

'I'm taking the car out shortly. I'll have a look round.' I breathed out softly. She had not been in the garage. I went over to the coffee pot, not wanting to sit with her. 'By the way, Maisie's here. She's in the spare room.'

'Is she?' she said, her voice rising.

'Yes. I saw her last night in the pub. She's been back a day or two. Things haven't been going too well up there, as far as I can gather. She hasn't really said much, but I'm sure she will, when she's ready.'

Mother looked dismayed, as if this was confirmation of something she already knew. Had she heard Maisie and me talking? Or had Maisie been crying while I was away? 'Sounds odd,' she said.

I brought her coffee and stood with my own drink, leaning against the wall. What was I doing there? I never stood there. And the familiar old kitchen had a different air, with its white-tiled and white-glossed walls, Andy's clattering of cutlery making it feel like some kind of institution, a school or a hospital. I was detached from its true relationship to me. Everything was so light and unreal. 'I'll be going soon,' I said. 'I've a few things to do.'

'What time will you be back?'

'Soon enough. Lunchtime probably. Don't worry, Mary'll get away on time.'

Mother sipped the coffee, the mug held between the gold-ringed fingertips of both hands. 'Could you drop into the chemist's for me? My leg was hell last night.' She rubbed her hip, flinching for effect. 'Felt like it was on fire. I'm sure there's an infection.'

'Don't you need a prescription for something like that?' I said, too sharply.

'No. I just want a bottle of that, what's it called – '

'Couldn't Mary go?' The irritation had seeped into my voice.

She wrinkled her bottom lip and scratched behind her ear. 'Well, I suppose so. I just thought that while you were out, you could get it.'

It was already going wrong. My trip out this morning was assuming an unnecessary significance. I should have cleared off without saying anything. A few excuses later would have explained it well enough. 'What I mean is,' I said, blushing hopelessly, 'I may be a while. If you're in pain, you might as well have the stuff now.'

It was like schooldays. Mother knew I was hiding something. She shrugged. 'All right.'

I put my mug in the sink. 'I have to go. I'll send Mary in.'

I went to the lobby. Mary was behind the desk in her dowdy black uniform and white lace cap. In her maddening old woman's way, she was tidying papers that didn't need to be tidied. 'There's been a complaint,' she said, squinting at the sheaf of food dockets in her hand. 'Mr Holding wants a word with you. His radiator wasn't working last night.'

I looked at the open dining-room door. The couple were sitting near the kitchen end. Mrs Holding glanced up at me and tapped her husband's wrist. 'It'll have to wait.'

'He's having breakfast. Couldn't you see him now?'

'No.' I was heading for the front door.

She put the papers down, mildly indignant. 'It would only take a minute.'

'I said no. I'll deal with it when I get back. Right?'

She looked away, offended. I had meant to put on a show of icy calm, and had only succeeded in upsetting everyone. 'I'm sorry. I'm in a bit of a hurry. I promise I'll see to it later. Give them another room if they want it.'

Mary did not like this idea. It was an affront to my late father's philosophy that all complaints should be dealt with promptly and courteously. But I could not pander to her any longer. 'My mother's asking for you. I think she wants you to run an errand. Will you go and see what she wants?'

'Yes, sir,' she said with a sarcastic curtsey.

I turned my back on her, went out of the main door and back down the side of the hotel to the garage. And without looking back at the kitchen window, where I imagined they were all standing watching me, I unlocked the double doors.

9

I closed one of the doors to block the view from the kitchen. Mother had been right. The dog too. There was a smell, a faint organic musk mingling with the usual odours of oil and dust. I looked at the parcel shelf through the back window of the car and checked underneath for seepages, finding nothing. I decided not to open the boot. It felt useful to consider Guy as merely an object, like an unwanted piece of furniture to be furtively dumped somewhere that morning. With such a displacement of the horror of it all, I could succeed.

Aware that either Mother or Andy might be watching, I worked quickly. At the back of the garage I found the spade and an old pickaxe I did not know we possessed. There was a roll of dusty black polythene for which I might find a use. I looked hurriedly about the shelves on the far wall, the half-empty tins of paint, car polish, the antifreeze I had put there myself. Ted, our once-a-month gardener, had left half a sack of compost in the corner, bits and pieces of garden cane, green plastic netting. But no quicklime. Maybe I would not need it? I remembered a case twenty years ago of a burnt-out car being found on the moors, the result of a love triangle, its occupant identifiable only by a bracelet. Couldn't I take the oil and burn the body in its hole before I covered it over? Now that I was on the move, the possibilities for disposing of human remains seemed numerous. And, like Colin with his morbid ruminations, we all knew something about the subject. What kind of society was it that traded so happily in this sort of information?

I had been in there for three or four minutes. I was dithering. Mother might come, or Andy, poking around on the pretext of bringing rubbish out to the bins. I opened the door to the back seat of the car. A riper whiff was loosened, fruity, catching in my throat. I took the can of oil and put it on the floor behind the front passenger seat together with the tools, the polythene, my boots and a pair of webby worn gardening gloves. I covered the little heap with my old coat and looked at my watch. Ten past eight. In three hours it might be over. Two minutes later, I was away.

The shops opened early on a Saturday. The tables outside Queenie's the greengrocer were laden with apples, peppers, cabbages. At a fancy-goods shop, a man was optimistically dragging out plastic barrels filled with toy cricket sets, windmills for sand castles, the remnants of last year's stock. Away from the main streets were the tat shops with windows full of toilet-roll pyramids, baskets of cheap underwear, retailers of an indeterminate nature selling stock cleared from bigger stores and factories inland. Then, walking past the war memorial, I saw Colin, bag in hand, about his Saturday-morning rounds. 'Bastard.' I whispered the word, concentrating on the road, trying to avoid his look. He seemed preoccupied and did not see me. I drove on over the railway crossing, past the Trawlerman's and out of town, feeling easier.

The morning was brightening up, the clouds breaking, a few touring caravans heading for a site a mile to the north of town, and cars and camper vans out to take advantage of the fact that the clifftop car parks were not yet charging their seasonal tariff. The driving relaxed me. At the hotel I had been on the verge of ranting at everyone. But that episode was over now and I need not think about it. Then it dawned on me that it would be stupid to attempt to set fire to the body. The fats might burn for hours, and the smoke coming from the trees would be seen for miles, causing all kinds of excitement. Such an act was beyond my experience. I would have to keep it simple but thorough. It had to be that. I must give it my all. I turned off the Oughton Road and onto the dual carriageway that ran parallel to the coast as far as the North York Moors. Half a mile ahead was a roundabout with a garage and a new small development of out-of-town stores. One of them was a DIY place. Was this a lucky find? Might they sell quicklime? Had I the time? At the roundabout I turned onto the road towards the new estate.

The sunshine had drawn a trickle of shoppers. I filed into the car park and pulled up on the empty row at the back. I checked the back seat and got out. On my way into the store I felt for the money in my pocket. It would be more than enough, surely. I went through the automatic doors and picked up a basket, trying to give myself that faintly bored expression of a male shopper.

At the far airy end of the store was a section marked 'Building Materials'. I walked along the aisles of plywood and chipboard sheets, paving slabs, yellow plastic pipes. At the end I was alone among ceiling-high scaffold shelves stacked with bags of cement, sand, ready-mixed concrete. But no quicklime. I stalled. Suddenly the place seemed too large and light. The words of a song came into my head – *All I wanna do, I know it ain't right, But all I wanna do,*

Is make lo-o-ve to you . . . It was something I had heard in the pub last night. It had lain there, despite all that had gone on since, a deposit in the folds of my brain. I felt dizzy, the exertions of the last nine hours catching up with me. It was too warm. The dry air was parching my throat. A floor buffer started up somewhere nearby. *All I wanna do . . .* I closed my eyes, feeling I could catch a moment's sleep on my feet.

'Having problems?' An assistant was standing six feet away, an oldish man in the bright-orange uniform of the store.

'I think I'm in the wrong spot. I was looking for the garden section.' The steadiness of my voice surprised me, but his look was smug, a knowingness in the eyes and leathery-lipped smile. He knew there was something wrong.

He laughed. 'You've come through it to get here!' He held his hands open in a gesture of contempt. 'That way. Back along the main aisle, to the left.'

'Thank you.'

'You're welcome,' he said emptily, the phrase probably foisted on him in staff training.

I went back between the scaffold shelves. At the end I turned. He was still watching me, grinning, waving his arm in the direction I should take. If he served a hundred customers that day, he would probably remember me, the first of the morning, a bit of an idiot. I smiled and nodded, compounding the air of a wimpish male, out of place in this, the world of the artisan.

The dizziness had passed. This was stupid. A perfunctory mistake. I had been here for ten minutes, visible to dozens of people. I had to get out. But, in case the man was still watching behind me, I carried on down the aisle and into the garden section. For effect, I would have to buy something before I left. In front of me were columns of biodegradable plant pots, bottles of fertiliser, bubble-wrapped hosepipe extensions. On the bottom shelf was a neat row of garden lime. Was that the same as quicklime? A weaker derivative perhaps, for the domestic market? I picked up a box and read the label: *For the rapid breakdown of all clay soils. Avoid skin contact.* I put it back and looked further along the shelf. There were more expensive brand names of the same substance. Would they be too refined? *Avoid skin contact* . . . I went back to the stuff I had seen first and put two heavy boxes in my basket. In a panicky moment, to make the purchases look less obvious, I added two pink heather shrubs from a display at the end of the aisle.

At the end of the row of checkouts was a security camera. Why hadn't I thought of that? Suddenly, everything looked too clear, the stark white walls at the end of the store, my hand around the basket handle. I kept my head low, pretending to be mesmerised by my purchases. Only two of the tills were in use and I had to take the one directly beneath the camera. The assistant lugged one of the boxes onto the counter and pointed her bar-gun at the code. I was looking down at the curls on her head, the arch of her back beneath the orange overall. She repeated the procedure. The price would not register on the till. She tried tapping in a number from the side of the box. Still nothing. Sweat was forming on my temples. I saw myself making an imbecilic apology and running, leaving the things where they were.

'Do you know how much it is?' the girl asked.

'I'm not sure.' I cursed myself for this oversight, my amateurishness laid bare and shaming. 'Would it be £12.99?'

'I'll have to go and look.'

She locked the till and shuffled off her stool. While she

was gone, a woman came up behind me. I kept my eyes averted, puffing my cheeks to make a show of annoyance at being delayed. The girl came back. '£7.45.'

'Really?'

'Do you want a bag?' She was tapping the buttons on the till.

'I can manage. Thank you.' I paid, took my change and left, cradling the things in my arms.

Outside, the sweat cooled on my temples and the hook of my jaw. From now on I would avoid all human contact until this was over. I headed for the car, then stopped ten yards short. The row that had been empty fifteen minutes ago was now half-full. At the car next to mine, a white Nissan, a young couple were loading up their boot from a shopping trolley. A small girl was with them, trying to balance on the kerb on the edge of a newly shrubbed border. I walked purposefully, almost angrily, up to the car, opening the passenger door and putting the boxes and heathers on the seat. But a small change in the car's interior symmetry caught my eye. The parcel shelf had lifted and the sun was catching a delta of grey forehead, a wisp of brown fringe. The girl was behind my car. Her head was bouncing up and down along the line of the tilted shelf and the rear window. She slipped off the kerb, tried the act again, then gave up, heading my way, skipping between the two vehicles.

10

She stopped level with the back wheel, wrinkling her nose. 'This car's horrible. It stinks.'

The father looked over, a pack of ceramic tiles in his hands. 'Yeah, well, come away.' He was about twenty-five, wearing a white T-shirt and jeans. He leaned into the trolley for another pack. As the blood rushed into my face, I thought I would trust this man. He was fed up. He was thinking about how he used to spend his Saturdays in the pub with his mates, or taking a train to the football. Before he got married, before this home-improving, nest-building shit.

'But it's awful!'

'Just leave it, will you?' He slammed down the boot and came round to pick her up, standing four feet from the top of Guy's head. The girl grimaced in his arms. He looked at me. 'Sorry, mate.'

I offered a weak smile. 'Not to worry.'

He turned to put the girl on the back seat of his car, fastening the seat belt around her. I pushed down the front passenger seat on the pretext of transferring the lime and plants to the back, picking up my coat to make space, throwing it on the parcel shelf to cover the raised end. The girl was watching from under the man's stomach, looking puzzled, turning to say something to her mother who was in the front of the car. I told myself she had not seen anything, at least nothing that would be believed. I imagined the father, a fine man, saying she was a silly girl who shouldn't say things that might upset a stranger. I went round to the other side of the car, got in and drove away.

And my mind flipped.

. . . I am in a shop in London, perhaps Chelsea. It sells things made of wax. Nicola is next to me, wearing her smart houndstooth jacket, the elegant oxblood court shoes. I am bored, waiting for her. 'If only I didn't have to choose!' she says, watching a burning candle decoration twirling on a plastic pool filled with water. The light catches her face, shadows on the skin, making her swarthy. 'If I could just take everything!' She turns, arms outstretched, looking about the shelves, beaming at the pastel-coloured figurines, the stacks of chunky square candles.

'We wouldn't have room,' I say. 'We'd be sick with the smell.'

'Tush! You're such a killjoy. Just be happy, can't you?'

There's something in her look, a dulling of the eyes. I am depressing her spirit. I am northern and heavy. I love her so much, but I don't know how to say it, how to drag the same feeling out of her. She picks a pale-green wax cat. 'You're lovely!' And two saffron roses. Pays for them.

Outside she is smiling but unsatisfied. The purchases may remain in their brown paper wrapping for months. Because she could not have everything. Because I cannot not satisfy her and tell her how much I want her . . .

The minute of madness passed. A tic of the brain, the stress of the moment. I did not want to think of Nicola, but to help the time along I promised myself I would try and find her when all this was over. It was a released need.

It would be my reward. There had to be something at the end of this, a gift for me.

I kept looking down at the steering wheel, the sunlight picking out twinkling atoms on its plastic surface. I felt my hair. It was as if I had just been sick, then I was sane again, after a fashion.

Somehow, the body had moved. Was it the jolting of the car? Had rigor mortis set in, forcing the limbs to straighten? Had the tissues inflated? The smell was stronger than before, though surely it was too soon for the process of putrefaction. Meat, of whatever variety, kept for longer than twelve hours in this temperature. The smell rattled me. I wound the window down to clear the air. Every half-minute I checked that the coat was still covering the raised end of the shelf. A coach overtook me, its passengers able to look down into the car. Wouldn't I be safer on the side roads? I wiped a little grease from the corners of my mouth. The stop at the store had been foolish. I felt weak, with everything still to do. The pain below my ribs was generalising to a larger, dull ache. I was thirty-nine years old and in bad shape. The effort ahead might kill me. Yet my indifference to this possibility was curiously healthy.

Two miles on, I turned up a quiet narrow road that linked the carriageway with Hastow and North Carnham, two tiny villages in the middle of nowhere. It was a road used mostly by the locals since it only led back to a main road that linked up with the dual carriageway three miles further on. The first half-mile was all farmland, but I could already see the wood I had in mind. I did not want to get there. I had no business there. It was trespass. People like me stayed on the main roads, pursuing their consumerist unrural existences. And I enjoyed driving. I could do it all day long. Did I have to stop? Couldn't there be, in this hi-tech world, some simpler, more efficient way of getting rid of someone? As the wood came closer, my stomach bubbled. There was water in my rectum. Diarrhoea. I was going to shit myself. *All I wanna do, I know it ain't right* . . . I blocked the tune from my mind, only to have it replaced by the pinging of the Mighty Wurlitzer: *I should be so lucky, lucky lucky lucky* . . . Then I remembered the letter. *She's good, Harold, in case you didn't know it. She's very good* . . . It shredded my hopes of a reconciliation. The cow! Was all this because of her, the way I had acted so rashly last night? Had the rage I had swallowed found another way to the surface? Was that my revenge loaded up in the boot, being delivered for interment? Did this really have anything to do with protecting a niece I barely knew? I reached the first of the trees.

I pulled up on the short track that led into the wood. I did not think I would stay. It seemed more likely I would drive away, back to Oughton perhaps, or on to Scarborough to a police station where I would hand them the keys of the car and rest, letting fate do as it would. The urgency in my bowels passed. That had been my one immediate problem. I felt calmer. Now I thought I could either drive on and give myself up, or I could bury Guy now and be home by the end of lunch. The two options lay before me. The tossing of a coin might be called for. I wound down the window at the passenger side, for the air, for a clear view of the wood. Its reality.

The five-barred gate to the wood was closed, but there was no sign of a lock. There were tyre marks up to the gate which gave the impression of its being used as a turning point, or a place for lovers to steam up the windows. Beyond the gate, the track was grassy, a green lane to the centre of the trees. It was National Trust territory. There would be an inspector or warden of some kind who would keep a check on the place. But that couldn't be more than two or three times a year. And surely not Saturdays? I got out of the car. The breeze was delicious, blowing in from the sea, three miles east. I was incapable of choice. There should have been someone to tell me what to do.

The road I had come along was clear, though further on I could pick out the top of a white van coming over a hill between the fields, three-quarters of a mile away. I went down the little dip and opened the gate reflexively, not a thought in my head. I could smell the damp earth, the air filtering through the trees. The sparrows were making their crunching chirps in the lower branches. I went back to the car and drove it through to a grassy recess forty yards along the track. I walked back and closed the gate, indifferent to being seen, being caught. By the time I had returned to the car, out of sight of the road, I heard the white van whoosh past the gate. It was a sign. I had tempted the fates and won. I had been winning all morning, a lucky streak it would be perverse to tamper with. I looked around, tucked my shirt in my trousers, opened the back door of the car and took the spade from behind the seat.

11

It was a place where Matthew and I would come on our bikes, perhaps with friends, other children of the coast for whom the sea had little fascination, its appeal burned out of us in natural-history lessons with the dry classification of shells and rocks, the naming of different types of seaweed. Here we might find wildernesses and the imagined hauntings of the moors further up, evidence of weird inland goings-on from which we were isolated.

The layout appeared miraculously unchanged, save for the maturity of the pines and the thick border growths of young hazel and sycamores. Fifty yards on, the track petered out. To my right the first pine trunks were thinly spread, but not far in I could see the dense centre of the wood. There could be few quieter places. Yet it felt too obvious, the choice of someone who had given no more than two seconds' thought to the practice in which I was about to be engaged. An open field might have been smarter. But it was too late for second thoughts. Decisiveness was the key. I put on the wellingtons and gloves, bunched up my coat over the parcel shelf, and set off through the swishing grass to the shadows of the trees.

Within twenty yards, I was out of sight of the car. I crouched to feel the soil beneath its carpet of dead leaves and brown pine needles. It was black and powdery, staining the fingers like soot. Baby ferns were growing everywhere. I stabbed at the ground with the spade. It went in to halfway up the blade. I began to feel grimly in tune with the task, forgetting the earlier reservations. And at the back of my mind was a glimmer of true hope. This might be over more quickly than I had imagined. I pressed on, my eyes getting used to the brown gloom. The wind was brushing the top of the wood, but the air around me was still and moist. A little further on I found a fallen pine. To the left was a soft hollow covered by a thin lattice of leafless wintering brambles. I drew back the brambles and leaves to make a clear oval area. I looked around. Everywhere else the trees seemed closer together, gathered for company, watching. This would have to do. I put on the gloves and began digging.

The first foot was soggy black topsoil followed by a thin stratum of chalky sand. I started at one side of the clearing with the aim of digging a small hole to sufficient depth which I would then enlarge by lifting out the side soil in strips. But after the sand came dense orange clay which I could penetrate only by stabbing with the spade, loosening it into cubes which were so small I was better off lifting them out with my hands. Despair put in a brief appearance. Bodies were found in shallow graves. It was a hackneyed yet true enough fact. The deep pit I had in mind would take days. It had been another of my asinine assumptions. But I carried on, deciding to make the hole to the length and breadth that was needed, laying bare the clay which I might assault with the pickaxe.

After fifteen minutes I had a roundish hollow, eighteen inches deep at most, with the clay and soil in lumpy heaps around the sides. Along the hole's centre, like a spine, ran a formidably thick tree root. Other, smaller roots protruded from the sandy layer, and even the thinnest took four or five stabs with the blade to cut away. It was a feeble scar on the face of the earth. An unmanly effort. Nowhere near enough. I rested for a minute, my chest raw, muscles hot with an exertion the likes of which I could not remember. The science of gravedigging flashed through my mind, the six-foot holes in churchyards. How did they manage to make them so deep? Was it a consideration in the construction of churches to surround them with soft, diggable soil? A graveyard would have been an ingenious place to hide a body. Why hadn't I thought of that? Another three hours' work here would take me only a foot deeper. A shallow grave – the dead wife shovelled beneath a few inches of soil, hours after the fateful argument, the husband's red mist in its amber twilight afterglow, his lunatic task needing to be completed before the rage died. I did not have this anger. This was not directly my problem. And I had imagined applying myself methodically, cool in the pursuit of family duty. I wanted to do my best, better than if it had been for myself.

A scraping sound startled me. A searching breeze had funnelled through the trees, disturbing a young holly growing against the trunk of a lone big birch. The fear was like a reawoken sickness, an old sapping panic that rose and fell. I took off the gloves to cool my hands. A blister was already forming on the inside of my thumb. But there could be no turning back now. I blew on my hot palms and returned to work.

At the upper end of the hollow the clay was wetter, and I could pull out half a sticky spadeful at a time, which I wiped off against the log. It seemed wise to remove the easier stuff first, even though it took me away from my original design, and some way of shifting the harder clay might suggest itself with the progress I was making. There was a smear of mud on my forehead. My hair was soaked with sweat. It trickled on my eyelids. But I worked on without thinking what the hole was for, imagining myself to be a workman explaining to an apprentice how such a task might be most economically achieved. After a few minutes I had a decent thirty-inch depression to the damp side of the hollow. This was a proper hole with the clay and soil in a hearteningly large ridge at the upper end. It was the sort of handiwork that might be credited to a good navvy looking for pipes beneath the ground. Things were getting better.

I took out a few wedges of the drier clay, aiming to make a trench back to where I had begun. My grip on the spade felt surer and to combat the burning of my hands I tried different fingertip holds and a schematic rhythm for stabbing at the clay, using the weight of the falling spade. In my head I prattled on to the imagined trainee about the lore of spadework, the refinements of cutting and lifting. The growing crater was making me giddy, almost proud. I cut through the thin end of the big root, levered it out of its clay bed and twisted it to the side. This left a channel of broken clay on which I was able to capitalise, a thin trench that only needed to be widened at the sides to complete my work. The last obstacle now was a large stone which I dug around and prised carefully loose, the blade bending as I levered it out. It came away with a dry sucking noise and I bent down and heaved it to one side. The clay beneath the stone was a deep grey, impacted. The hole could not be dug any deeper by human hand. Even the pickaxe would not move more than the first few inches. I looked at my watch, allotted myself another ten minutes of furious digging, half of which was taken up with shovelling back the clay which

72

kept falling back in from the sides. Then I got out, threw the spade aside and headed back to the car.

The sound of my feet rustling through the leaves, the growing light and air, inspired an appreciation of the craziness of what I had been doing. I had been digging my way to hell. Now the wood seemed to be closing up behind me. It would be blissful not to have to go back. I emerged into the daylight, into a different time zone and level of rationality. I stood breathing heavily, the physical excesses catching up with me, making my arms and legs shake. A slew of depression threatened. I could still abandon the idea.

Then, from somewhere beyond the southern end of the wood, came the sound of gunshot. Once, twice. How far away was it? Half a mile? More? It might be a farmer shooting rabbits, or a poacher after the few stray grouse that had survived last season's shoot on the moors. I waited at the side of the car, hearing nothing more, wondering about my judgement. But the panic was rising, a pressure in my head that told me I must not stop. If I could get the body to the hole, the refilling might take no more than a few minutes. A single shot came again. It seemed a long way off, easily a mile. In the time it would take anyone to make up the distance between us, I could be finished and away. It had to be done now. I opened the boot, lifted the parcel shelf.

And Guy looked up at me.

12

The light was a deception. In my mind it was still night, permanently so. I could see the grass moving in tresses in the breeze, a sea of shimmering silver and green. The branches were swaying, a blackbird shot across the divide of the track. But the sounds were muted. I looked at Guy, the eyes upturned and creamy. There was the smell of shit and urine, the hum of a feral, cold young man. My head filled with a hot lightness and I retched at the side of the car, spitting out coffee, scraps of food I could not remember eating.

The nausea passed and the birdsong and rustling of the wood returned pin-sharp. I straightened up, hungry for fresh air, feeling better. The gunshots came again, muffled, still further away. It seemed fair to believe that whoever it was had no interest in the wood. I took another wholesome breath and brought the polythene sheet from the rear of the car. The action lent a calmer sense of purpose. I was nearly forty years old. There was a limit to what I could physically achieve. A more considered, gentler approach was needed for this final stage. I spread the sheet on the ground, standing on it to lean into the car.

The body was stiff, but not rigidly so. In its reality, rigor mortis seemed to have a less extreme quality than

I had imagined. One of Guy's bloodied hands was stuck under the frame of the back seat and I had to force the arm down to tug it free. I rolled the body towards me, shuffling it around to get one arm under the shoulders, the other under the knees. The odours stirred and I put my head to the side to take in air. Now I was cradling him the same way as when I had dropped him inside. I dug my heels into the slippery polythene and heaved him up to the lip of the boot. The blood on his overshirt was drying, thick as oil. It had seeped out and gathered on his back and buttocks. There was a faint cloud of pink on the grey carpet lining the boot. I leaned over to get a grip on his back and for a horrid split second I imagined he might suddenly come kicking to life in my arms, an angry youth bawling about the way he had been treated. I dismissed the notion and let him roll out, dodging back as he dropped, his hand and hips slapping on the sheet. The action encouraged me. I was dealing with an inanimate object, a dead thing I need not fear. I closed the boot.

Originally I had thought of wrapping the body in the polythene and dragging it over to the hole. It would have minimised the need to touch it. But there was barely enough to cover him and the undergrowth would have ripped the polythene. I would have to lift him the whole way there. I pulled the ruffled sheet from under him and covered the head and upper body. A few vague rules about lifting heavy objects came to mind – keeping a straight back, using your legs to take the weight. But I disregarded them, clenching my jaw, crouching over and picking him up. I had him around the waist and shuffled him higher, swaying, top-heavy with the load. There was certain to be an easier way. But this was a journey that would only have to be made once.

The trip back to the hole took less than a minute. Guy

was slipping out of the polythene, but I did not rest. I was feeling frail, though the retching seemed to have rid my body of some toxin. At the hole I lowered him down on the inside of one of the smaller piles of soil and clay, tugging the polythene from beneath him. He slithered in, rolling on his back.

I had guessed the size of the hole reasonably well, though one shoulder was too high and the knees were up. When covered, they would be no more than six inches from the surface. I got down in the hole, straddling him, tugging him into the centre of the depression, pressing down on his knees. But they were firmly locked, as if exposing the body to fresh air had abruptly hastened the process of stiffening. I lifted him to the side, so he was sitting watching me as I retrieved the spade and dug away a small recess, tailoring the bottom of the hole for the shoulders. Now it was tempting to just push him down again, shovel back the clay and soil, and go. But there was his clothing to remove and I still had the lime to consider. It might work. And I had made such an effort to get it. One more ounce of patient activity could prove priceless. I pushed Guy back, pressing his limbs into the clay. Then I stood beside the hole, gathered up the polythene and looked down at him. My burden was in place. The hardest part was over. I set off back for the car, breaking into a run with a second wind born of the elation that I was no more than fifteen minutes away from getting this over with. But when I emerged from the trees I stopped.

A man was making his way out of the wood at the far end of the track, a shotgun broken over his arm. He was ambling across, glancing up at the higher branches, looking ahead at me.

The self-satisfaction disappeared. The wreckage of my

folly was all about me, the polythene sheet, the trampled grass. I might as well have signposted the way to Guy's body. The man came closer. He was about to suffer the most wretched experience. I bundled up the sheet and tossed it on the back seat, closing the door when he was just ten yards away. He came up to the car. I saw myself driving us both to the police station. I could not put him through the misery of a struggle. And he had a gun, though something told me he would not dare use it on a human being. My eyes were warm, tears of exasperation ready to flow.

'Morning!' he said.

I wiped my forehead to get rid of the dirt, and in a vague attempt to show I was tired. 'Good morning.' I gestured towards the bundled-up polythene on the back seat. 'A bit of leaf mould for the garden.' A pathetic excuse, but to my surprise he nodded, as if the story was perfectly acceptable.

'Aye, well. Good stuff here. Good thick loam. A bit acid maybe, you know, the pine needles and that.'

'Yes.' I smiled excessively. 'That's what I thought.'

He was fiftyish, tall and drop-shouldered, wearing a wax coat and battered hat. He did not have the possessive look of a farmer or game warden. In fact there seemed a certain wariness in the eyes, the limp set of his mouth. Might he be from one of the villages that dotted the area? One of those old inbred families that had been here for centuries, poor and resentful of the property-owning classes, after anything they could steal from the land? They were still like that round here, I was sure, more so in these days of chronic unemployment.

'Are you hunting?' A remark on the offensive. Maybe he would think I had something to do with the place.

He shrugged, saying nothing, stealing a quick and

obvious glance at the unused pickaxe in the back of the car. He hitched up the gun in his folded arms, looking round along the way he had come. 'Bad track this. Go any further and your wheels'll get stuck.'

I laughed casually. 'Yes, I know. I was about to call it a day anyway. I've got all I want.'

The man was thinking. Now I was annoyed with him, his meddlesomeness. I hated it here, this part of the country with these small-minded people and their piddling existences. He took a few steps towards the path I had made through the grass. I did not move. From where he was now, he might spot the sick at the side of the car. But if he did, he took no notice of it. He looked up into the trees and along the roadward length of the track. 'Bit of rain later, I think.'

'Do you reckon?'

'It's possible.' He made a clicking noise with his tongue, spat on the grass, and turned to me with a nod. 'Well, I'll be seeing you.'

'Yes.'

'Cheerio, then.'

'Yes. Goodbye.'

He stepped back across the track and disappeared into the other half of the wood. I waited a few seconds before hiding the pickaxe under the sheet, making a show of activity for anyone else who might be watching. A minute later, from somewhere in the trees, came a gunshot. It sounded like an expression of anger. But it was far enough away. I took the boxes of lime from the car and went back to the hole.

Guy was looking up at the sky. It was as if he was quietly contemplating the heaven that was beckoning. I had no feeling left for him. I had become so used to handling his body that I was beyond the grotesqueness of it, a seasoned manipulator of the dead. Had it been a job, it might have paid well.

I set the boxes down between two ridges of clay and got into the hole, again straddling the body. I took off his trainers and socks and unfastened the jeans. By prising the knees apart, the jeans and pants came off fairly easily, revealing the dark purple of his feet and shins, unhealthily narrow hips, the dead white worm of his prick in its bush of pubic hair. But the sweatshirt was more of a problem. The arms were locked together. The shirt came up to his neck but could not be pulled over the head. I tugged hard but it would not move. I lifted up the T-shirt underneath to see if they might roll off together, but they bunched up in a thick rope behind his neck. I rested a few seconds, seeing the black wound on his chest, the milky skin covered in clay smears and streaks of dried blood. Then I noticed a lattice of small scratches and a second incision, an inch below the first. Had he been stabbed twice? Maisie had not mentioned this. Maisie . . .

There was a sweet smell. Not perfume. The gas of the soil. And of the body, thick in my nose. Dead meat. I could not think straight. I couldn't take it any more. And profanity followed, an evil I did not think I was capable of, as I pulled at the ravelled shirts one more time and kicked Guy's head to try and get it through. The act loosened my agitation. I began booting Guy's head and face. Because I wanted to. This was personal, satisfying, the exorcism of some unspecifiable grievance against the human race. I did it again, relishing its cathartic element, the thud of my heel on his cheeks, mouth and the plate of his forehead. Again and again, the attempt at removing his clothing forgotten. After a minute, I stopped and let him drop on his back. His face and chest were covered in my boot marks, his lips torn, an eyebrow split in the centre. I climbed out of the hole and ripped open one of the boxes, my hands shaking.

Inside the box was a clear plastic bag containing the fine white powder. I ripped it open and sprinkled the lime all over the body, repeating the act with the other box, thickening the frosted covering. I threw the boxes aside, pushed the big root over Guy, and weighed it down with the large stone. Then I took the spade and shovelled back the clay and topsoil, not looking down into the hole.

Within minutes, the area was flat. I trampled it down. It gave a little before settling. But I had had enough. I swept dead leaves over the ground and pulled back the brambles. For a few seconds more, I scuffed up my footprints with the spade before picking up the clothes and boxes and running back to the car where I sat inside, grinning madly. Then I wept, a dry affair, and knew why we spend our lives in flight from all that is painful and real.

PART TWO

13

When the heat came, the television sets did not work. To the guests, my mother said, 'The atmospherics.' She repeated it time after time, pleased with having this response, its brief simplicity. The sun was there from late April to mid-May, an unseasonal heat wave interrupted only by a three-day spell of wind and slanting heavy rain. During the worst of this, three tankers came in off the North Sea to shelter in the bay, and a ruinous tide swept away chunks of the already disappearing Head. Otherwise the visitors still came, the families with shopping-bag-laden pushchairs, the jet-skiers and sailors, old people on the promenade with their walking sticks and the white sunhats they bought for a pound apiece off the market. The scarlet awning above the Finlandia's door was washed and polished, and Mother, with Ted's help, decorated the forecourt, filling her little white decorative barrow with red geraniums, putting up hanging baskets of lobelia, posting the potted palm by the door where it would stay till November. And each morning I put the white plastic chairs and tables outside to talk up the hope for a good summer, that annual, tediously voiced concern of all who came to the coast. Yet the work at the Finlandia kept me going. It was good for me. It helped to stop me thinking about what I had done.

We were full for most of Easter and managed to attract plenty of bookings for the crucial months of July and August when the hotel made its living for the year. With bolder advertising, I thought we could have filled the place for the season and beyond. But that was not how things were done in Oughton and I did not want to interfere with its languid ways. Besides, what did I know? I, Harold Broome, erstwhile owner of the Chandelier Restaurant in Deptford, who had done this kind of work all his life, flitting from job to job, bed to rented bed, whose one venture alone had ended in bankruptcy in less than a year? My life, in short. A shade aimless, though not unhappy. In other circumstances, a return to the place of my growing-up, in my fortieth year, might have been a good time for mature reflection on what I had done with my life. And there was something to be learned from Oughton's air of apology, its flinching wisdom which I had known all my life, yet had never given it credit for. But such a résumé was beyond me, and I was pleased just to watch the weeks pass, the people coming and going without troubling me.

Of Guy, there was not a word. I am not a psychologist, nor much of a believer in such sciences, but there was some kind of protective displacement at work in my mind. The act I had performed that weekend was so momentous that I could not think about it if I tried. I was denying it, I knew, yet it was the only way I could carry on living. The few waking concessions I did make to my memory of the event included my hiding of the tape of the Mighty Wurlitzer, which unsettled me, and the fact that I persuaded Colin to change our Friday-night venue to the White Rose, whose quiet taproom was a relief to him, while for me it meant an avoidance of the place where I had met Guy. At Easter we began taking the newspapers for the guests and I examined every one of them, with an unspeakable apprehension at the turn of every page. But after a month or so I allowed myself the belief that no one had missed Guy, or that he was not worth a place in the news.

I worked the bar and avoided thinking about Guy by only thinking about myself, fences and walls built against the demands of others, identifying my wants, developing appetites for only the things that pleased me and let my mind sleep – reading, long hours in front of the television, when it worked, occasional walks on the cliffs with the dog, a graded pattern of drinking that began at eight and carried on until I was satisfied. An avoidance, yes, of all that was too painful and real – no more worrying about the next day, no more waiting to want for the things that might make me happy, however minute or mundane. It could have been my age, the onset of that famously exacting midlife crisis. But I did not want to believe in such a thing. I desired only complacency, a means for letting my subconscious work out on its own the horror of those two March days. And I thought of the three anglers who had drowned that winter, three miles off the bay. Two brothers and a friend. I did not know them, I did not care about them. What was life but a pulse of energy, disappearing in a puff? A few hundred good meals, sex, money, the boozy oblivions. Did it amount to much more than that? A callous way of thinking, but it helped. Otherwise, the event that was Guy was a lost lump of time, though the details, as I smiled for our guests and ruffled the hair of their children, were still there, in all their clarity at varying depths beneath the surface.

When I got back to the hotel that Saturday, Maisie was up, wearing the clothes she had been out in the night before, talking in the kitchen with Mother, making too much of a fuss of Kipper. She was forcedly cheerful, manic-eyed with fatigue. When I managed to get her alone in my room, I told her, 'It's done. Now all you have to do is forget about it.' A shadow passed through her, the trauma still at work, raw and gnawing. She couldn't forget. Guy's things were still in the house. The tears came without notice. And there was a wish to confess, to cleanse herself. It was not her fault, I said. If Guy hadn't attacked her, he would have attacked someone else. He was a type, a waster. It was his fate to end up the way he did. The argument was clichéd. I was talking down to Maisie, wanting to put words in her mouth. My coldness frightened her, but it had to be so. I was throwing open the door on an aspect of adulthood, its hypocrisy, which she did not like the look of, but had to pass through.

Later that afternoon, having asked Lionel to come in and look after the bar for a few hours, I took Maisie back to the house. It was a gamble. I was being hard, yet it seemed right to get her involved in some way, to desensitise her. Together, we bleached the kitchen floor. I wiped door handles with a damp cloth and scrubbed away the smudges of blood in the back yard, hoping for a hard frost that might sterilise it completely. Maisie collected Guy's things together in a black bin bag. I put the knife in an envelope and kept it in my pocket. The effort was good for both of us. We were working around the incident, diminishing it with physical activity. And when we had finished, Maisie seemed cooler, hands clasped and smiling, reinforcing my hope that what we had done was right. She packed a bag with clothes and came back to the Finlandia. That night she sat talking in the bar with Mother, sharing her cigarettes. And the next morning I took all of Guy's belongings, his watch, the polythene sheet and my stained shirt, and burned them in our garden incinerator. I put the knife in too, making sure the wooden handle was burned away, fishing out the blackened blade and hammering it into an unrecognisable shape. At dusk I took that and every scrap of ash, scorched metal buttons and zippers, to an outcrop on the far side of the Head, where I dumped it on the strong ebb tide.

Naturally, Maisie could not go back to Newcastle. She spun Mother a tale of poor lodgings, a friendless existence, laying it on thick about an overdemanding course, though Mother seemed to accept it all without question. Then, after a week of doing nothing, Maisie was suddenly spurred to activity, ringing Matthew to explain what was going on, calling on her friends in Oughton, and finding a place at Nottingham where she could pick up her studies. She had to get away. It was obvious.

She went after Easter. I took her to the station. We did not mention Guy, but the subject was there between us, so large and tantalising that we had to avoid it. What a pair we were, standing on the empty platform, by the flaking white walls of a provincial, loss-making station, smiling in embarrassment with this seismic secret on both our minds. I gave her a hug, the reassurance of a blood relation, my loyalty. She looked both brave and unconvinced, her breath shallow, brown hollows beneath the eyes, her youth eluding her, perhaps lost for good. And she was thin, shivering in a nonexistent breeze. I fretted over the loneliness I saw coming her way. There seemed no saving her from it. She would forget in time, I told myself. She had to. But the tears were flowing when she took her seat and waved from the moving train.

For the next few weeks I went about my business as usual, having to admit to myself that Maisie's departure was something of a relief for me. I could carry the problem alone, and it was easier that way as I went about my life, oddly alert to my responsibilities, taking greater pains to ensure the comfort of our guests, mindful of the feelings of the staff. In particular I tried to ingratiate myself with Lionel, developing a line in bawdy jokes, letting him off early on the quieter nights. It was pure sycophancy, but it smoothed the passage of the days. And I rang Maisie each weekend. The talk was only of her studies, the house she was sharing with four others, the merits of Nottingham night life. Time had put a film over what we had done. Its passing pleased me on a daily basis. I was living quietly, for a while hopeful of a future of growing old without excitement or complication. I was fitting in, becoming part of the furniture as I dealt with the laundry, worked out the food orders, laughed with the guests in the bar. My actions were detached, a soothing state in which the real Harold was, I believed, invisible to the world. Then one mid-May morning, a ghost came to trouble me.

I was in the kitchen, taking the morning break with Lionel. We were planning to clear out a storeroom on the first landing, a job conceived by me in which I intended to take on the lion's share of humping the discarded furniture down the stairs, making a show of the manliness he did not credit me with. Later, we would take the lot to the tip.

'The weather'll be all right this afternoon,' I said. 'Though you wouldn't think it, listening to the forecast. They always say it's colder on the east coast.'

'Everybody complains about that, Harold.' He was leaning against the sink, holding his empty cup, perhaps wanting to kill time, resenting this extracurricular activity. 'You want to write to them. Tell them it's bad for business.'

'I might,' I said, though I knew I would do no such thing.

'Yeah, well, you've got to fight your corner in this world. Otherwise the buggers'll trample all over you.'

He rinsed his cup, looking unusually introspective, the ex-soldier, a strong man who had flexed those heavy freckled biceps for his country. I imagined him drinking in the army mess, the crude cries for England and the Queen, sentiments too quaint for the ungrateful civilian masses, wankers like myself. And now he was now doing Mickey Mouse work, earning a boy's wages, with no future at all. He had a right not to like me. I put down my mug and was about to suggest that we made a start when the door creaked behind me.

'Harold?'

It was Mother, one hand on her stick, the other on the door handle. She had her look of matriarchal disapproval, cultured over three decades, the eyes hooded, the downy lips parted in distaste, a breathlessness thrown in for contemporary effect.

'There's someone to see you,' she said.

14

The calves, of course, I knew well. They were too straight, tubular, lacking that erotic curve to the heel. It was a surgically unalterable flaw that had always pained her. But the rest of her showed the usual careful attention. The black hair was shorter, centre-parted and lifted back, a few tresses straying up by design. I remembered the white jacket from one of her shopping trips in Knightsbridge. The ivory silk blouse might have been bought the same day. In profile, the mouth looked piquish, but she turned to me smiling, that prettily lazy left eye glinting.

'Hello, Harold.'

'Nicola.'

'I'm sorry. I should have phoned.'

I went behind the reception desk, wanting it as a line of defence while the kick of seeing her dissipated. 'Well, what brings you here?'

She shrugged, smiling, head to one side.

I gestured to her to come behind the desk. 'Come in the office. Would you like coffee? Or a drink?'

'Coffee would be lovely. Thank you.'

Mother was still in the doorway. I looked at her and she nodded, turning slowly into the kitchen to get Lionel to make up a tray for us.

In the office I sat at my usual place, but Nicola remained standing, reluctant to take the seat beside the desk in case it gave me territorial advantage – the interviewer, the interviewee. She leaned against the filing cabinet behind me, the window framing her head. The pose could have been deliberate, the high cheekbones outlined to greatest effect. My wife's beauty was a gambit she had played all her life, hourly, if there was something to be gained by it. She laughed suddenly. 'You know, this is a really pretty town. I never noticed before.'

'Did you drive here?'

'Set off at eight. Four hours. Not bad.'

'You came up from London?'

'Yes.'

I wished she would sit down. Lionel came in with the tray, taking a good look, eyeing her legs, happy with disbelief at my wife's arrival here. He winked at me before he left. I poured the coffee and Nicola sat on the edge of the chair at the side of the desk. She waved a cigarette. I pushed Mother's ashtray across. 'Nicky . . .' I took a deep breath and let it out. 'What do you want?'

She lit the cigarette, blowing smoke through a large, satisfied smile. 'I just wanted to see how you were. I was missing you.'

I closed my eyes, shaking my head. 'You were missing me?'

She tapped the cigarette on the ashtray, hand shaking, feigning nervousness. 'I wanted to know how you were. That's what I said, wasn't it?'

I reached for the coffee, not really wanting it. 'Well, I'm coping very well, thank you.'

'Good. That's good.'

The next few moments passed in silence. I sipped my

drink and put down the cup. She both was and was not the woman of my nightmares, my mental aberrations. 'Nicola, have you come to pull me to pieces again? Because I just can't stand that any more.' It was an immediate resumption of hostilities. My bluntness gratified me.

'No. Why should I?' The look of innocence was staggering.

'Then what's the reason? There's nothing new to say, as far I can see. The divorce is on its way, isn't it? Or are there more bills to pay?'

'No. There are no bills.'

'Well, give me a clue then.'

A man came up to the reception desk and rang the bell. Mother came from somewhere nearby to see to him. The door was still open a few inches. Nicola looked at it, listening to my mother's voice. 'Can we go for a walk or something?'

I was glad of her discomfort and of having a fine ally in my mother. 'Sure. Why not? I'll show you the sights. We didn't seem to manage it last time, if I remember rightly.'

'No,' she said. 'I don't think we did.'

It is two years ago, more or less. It is late at night at the Purple Tree Club in Lambeth. I'm waiting to go, tired, sick of the job, wanting another change. There are three City types, easing to laughter from the strain of whatever work they do. And there is a couple in the corner, both drunk. I have watched her for a while, the downcast eyes and determined anger. In my experience I know it will end badly, though I'm hoping it's not here. Then she dumps her drink on his head. He is stupid, he could have moved out of the way easily. But that is not part of the process. The men look up, the joking hardened to polite smiles, a glance in

92

my direction to suggest I should do something about this behaviour. But it's best to wait, patience the smarter policy in these situations – there is no damage to the premises yet, no one hurt, only one man's trampled pride.

When they leave, it is a relief for all. I am at the men's table, asking if they want a last drink, when she returns with a bloodied lip. 'What can you do about this?' she says. I take her into the empty dining room, switch on a corner light and fetch swabs and water. I dab at the split. 'Get me a drink.'

'I don't think it will help.'

'Let me decide that.'

I bring her another of the Bacardis she has been ordering, but she puts the glass down without drinking. A tiny droplet of blood seeps from the healing cut. She dabs it with the back of her hand, examining the smear on her skin with a cool eye.

'Kiss me,' she says.

'Look, really. It's getting late.'

'Kiss me.' She pulls me towards her. 'Make it hurt. I want you to.'

It was disarming, the two of us walking together. I could not remember Nicola ever wanting to walk anywhere. She had an abhorrence of exercise. Why did you learn to drive if it wasn't to give up the slowness, the childishness of getting about on foot? We went through the Rose Gardens and down to the promenade in silence, the warm sun climbing to its midday peak. The din of the town's one amusement arcade was carrying from the north end, borne by the wind. Three boys, wringing wet from running in the sea in their clothes, came running by, aggressively excited, foul-mouthed. Oughton's seediness laid before my wife's eyes. It pleased me. I wanted it seedier.

My many grievances against Nicola came to me in a flux, but the moment to offload them seemed some way off. Maybe I would end up saying nothing.

At the end of the promenade, we stopped. I could not imagine Nicola wanting to climb the rough path to the top of the cliff, and walking back would be pointless. I sat down on a bench near the town's last surviving row of beach chalets, and Nicola joined me in surprising obedience. I stared out at the sea. 'I got your letter.'

Nicola raised her chin seriously, as if she was the injured party. 'I'm sorry. It wasn't meant to be sent.'

'Do I know this fellow?'

'No. He's somebody from way back, when I used to work at the music shop I told you about. I needed the company. I was lonely. It was all a bit stupid, really.'

I sat forward, scraping the soles of my shoes on the sandy tarmac. People were passing in both directions and I looked in each of their faces, examining them because I could not bring myself to look at my wife. 'And are you seeing him now?'

'No. It was just a rebound thing. A mistake. One of my many.'

I let out a soft gasp. 'I'm supposed to sympathise with that, am I?' The anger was arriving, making my chest flutter. It might be unstoppable. 'Sometimes you're incredible, do you know that?'

'Harold, don't. I know I've been in the wrong and I want to apologise. I mean it.'

'That's a bit rich, Nicky.'

She pulled her jacket around her, folding her arms. It would have been easy to let fly at her, to tick off the list of injustices she had visited on me. But the impulse was off centre. It was as if I wanted her to go away so I could return to my fantasies about such a confrontation, ordering my words, ranting into the lonely night. It was a morbid, cowardly thing to wish for, but easier for me. Here, her physical presence forbade any directness.

Her name is Nicola Purley, the only offspring of the Purleys of Basingstoke who make electronic components for factory production lines and something obscure, something she can never be bothered to tell me about. Over the next few days she tells me her boyfriend was a creep, not like me, so honest, down to earth. A week later she moves into my flat. Two weeks after that we marry. She is fine for me, something from a dream, a quality creature, the likes of which I could only remember admiring from behind a counter. And the sex is raw, impulsive. She likes it hard and often. It is the new life I have wanted for a decade, a burning thing, life itself suddenly aflame, brilliantly unruly.

We buy a modest house in Deptford. She wants this smallness, for months this is all she wants, a tiny limited existence, a sitting and waiting consciousness while I work the days and nights at the Purple Tree and she knows I will be home for her when I have finished.

Then she says, 'I'm tired of being on my own. We have to be together the whole time, or it won't work. We have to eat together, fuck together, be with each other. I'm tired of your job. You don't come home enough. You're never at home. We love each other, don't we?'

And so it goes, so it went. What had I seen in her? Perhaps I was too set in my ways, old before my time. A bachelor, no history, no essence. I wanted this bruising immediacy, this joy. Was it my crisis? I will talk only of the business, the dry details. It is easier to describe than the pain of my feelings for her.

A year after we were married we raised a loan on the house, overstating its value, and opened our little English restaurant, next to a bike shop, off the High Street. Nicola was meant to supervise the cooking, using the college skills she undoubtedly had. But Nicola never stuck anything for long. This I had suspected, but did not want to admit. Within a week she was complaining of tiredness, and soon after the ladles were hitting the steel sink with an ear-splitting, tiresome ferocity. When the crockery began to fly in front of our bemused customers, I took on someone else, whom we couldn't afford. Nicola took to disappearing for days on end. She shopped, she spent. It was her way. The business never really started. Life before that, when I had been a bored and overworked deputy manager at the Purple Tree, seemed idyllic in comparison. When the business folded I tried to get my job back to keep up with the loan, but there was nothing doing. The debts seemed to breed, cancerously. 'I shall be a bankrupt,' I said. 'There's no other way.' Nicola could not take it, could not accept the embarrassment, the truth of the failure she had brought on us both. Maybe it was always going to end up the way it did.

And now, here we were on a bright May morning in my home town, strangers to those times and to each other. I wished she had not come.

An RAF helicopter was patrolling low over the edge of the tide, a life-jacketed, helmeted man standing perilously in its open side door, watching the people below. The sea was flat and silvery in the sunshine, hurting the eyes if you looked too long. But I kept looking, wanting it to burn up my many little pains.

'I've been a bitch to you, haven't I?'

'That's putting it mildly.'

'Look, Harold, you won't believe this, but I've come to realise what we had going for us – '

I laughed. 'Oh, don't, for God's sake.'

I looked at her, the thin crescent lines around the corners of her mouth, the delicate brown mascara, an expensive brand you wouldn't be able to buy in Oughton. I wondered if her father was funding her. 'Harold,' she said. 'Don't hate me.'

The helicopter was away to the south, a toy suspended in the air. Somewhere behind us, on the top crescent, there was a whippy-sounding hammer at work, echoing against a wall. On the beach, the wind was blowing the sand in sheets and devils, yet the walkers and joggers were there aplenty with their dogs chasing and fighting in the water. Closer in, a group of handicapped kids was trying to grasp the fundamentals of volleyball, their shouts and laughter dominating the area.

'I don't,' I said.

And I knew I could not hate her. The rage had passed. I had been seduced by her company as easily as the first time I had met her. I used to be so proud of being seen with her, walking round art galleries, sitting with her, newly wed, at street cafés in Paris. After years of flaky, unsatisfying relationships, guarding a freedom that turned out to be a lonely illusion, I was glad to marry her. There was her beauty, but there were other odd things, the letters that came bearing our two names, her coat in the hall, her wet footprints on the bathroom carpet. Her evidential presence sometimes seemed more important than the real one. It told me I was living with someone else, that I was a changed man. It was what I had needed. It gave me a sense of completeness. The restaurant was the end of it. But then, perhaps anything would have killed us off. 'What is it you want, Nicola?'

'I want us to think about trying again.'

I shook my head. 'It wouldn't work. We went too far. You couldn't stand it. We'd be at each other's throats within a week. Anyway, I'm a bankrupt. I couldn't support either of us.'

'That wouldn't matter.' She sat forward, her knee touching mine. 'You get paid for working here, don't you?'

'It's nothing. It depends on how well we're doing.' I turned to her. 'Nicola, I don't have any money.'

'Harold!' She looked genuinely hurt. 'That's not what I meant. What I'm saying is, think what you learned from the restaurant. You wouldn't make the same mistakes again.'

It amused me that she felt I thought so much about running my own business. I had done it to please her, for us both to be together. A vanity. 'I couldn't be bothered trying. I haven't the heart for it. And I'm needed here. Mother's not so good.'

She smiled. 'There'd be some way round that, surely. How would she have managed if you hadn't come back?' She shifted closer. 'I can get money.'

'You mean your father? I don't want anything from him.'

'He'd have bailed you out, if you'd asked.'

'It would've been throwing good money after bad.'

'God, you're so proud!'

'It's a failing.'

'It's lovely.' She took my hand. 'You're a nice man, Harold. And honest. Too honest for your own good.'

Again, this word 'honesty'. My fingers were limp in hers.

I liked her touch, yet it was wrong, too easily addictive. On the sands, one of the volleyball players had fallen and wrenched back her wrist. Her cries were yelping, beyond consolation. The young man and woman in charge attended to her, motioning to the others that they were abandoning the game.

'The poor thing,' said Nicola.

The sympathy was true enough. She really did like children, though she never talked about it. Had I been too dismissive of her barrenness? Was it really down to hormones, too many or too few millimoles per millilitre of something known only to women? Or was this a conceit of mine, a misogynism?

I squeezed her hand politely. 'Come on. We'll go back and have lunch.'

15

I watched her inspecting Mother's pictures in the bar, taking a good look round the lobby, tapping the barometer. She had some halting conversation in the kitchen with Mother, talk that ended with Nicola's dinner-party laughter. The two had never cared for each other.

I felt humble looking at my wife, the square set of her shoulders, the way she ran her finger along the edge of the reception desk. I thought back to our wedding, the registry office in Basingstoke where her parents lived, our two families standing dutifully on the steps for the photographer, Mother's accent grotesquely shrill as she tried to share niceties with Nicola's father. I could not remember seeing the photographs since a week or two after the wedding. I wanted to see them again, to remind myself that I was there, that it actually happened, that day with everyone filing into the room for the formalities, my father slim and ruddy and loud, probably already carrying the cancer that would kill him months later. Getting married seemed such a grown-up thing to be doing. Nicola's mother wept for the occasion. I wondered if she had done that when her daughter had married the first time round, nine years before. And I wondered what she thought of me now.

We took lunch in the office. My mood was lightening

with the wine. Soon I might reach that excitable plain from which the rest of my life looked needlessly difficult. That was when I did things I later regretted. Since the business with Guy, which I was still able to avoid thinking about quite brilliantly, I had been systematic with my drinking. But now, with the season of light nights and someone to drink with besides Colin and Mother, the urge to let go felt irresistible.

Nicola made a show of enjoying the modest meal of plaice and chips. She looked around the office. 'How long's this place been going?'

The interest was forced. I had told her all about the Finlandia before. 'Thirty-odd years.'

'That's a real achievement.'

'It was all the old man's doing. He had an eye for business. It was instinctive, a sort of Yorkshire thing.' I laughed. 'I'd probably have fouled it up if I'd been running the place.'

She lifted her glass. It was her third. She was already over the limit for driving. 'To the next thirty years!'

'Yes,' I said, swallowing a mouthful of fish and batter. 'Why not?'

When we had finished, and when I knew Mother would be in the bar talking to a smooth middle-aged couple she had taken a shine to, I suggested coffee in the upstairs flat, thinking to avoid my afternoon duties and lay the day to waste. Walking up the stairs and along the landings, I was head of the household, making comments about turnover, the little stories of the hotel's history, the woman who had died in room 7, the escaped convict who twenty years ago had passed through on the run from Hull prison, later to be caught in Scarborough. I mentioned the crippling bank rates, business talk, the sort of thing we might have indulged in when we had the restaurant, if Nicola had taken an interest. They were the things I had wanted to say that depressing weekend when I had brought her here before, when she had lain in bed and sulked, and hardly had a word for my parents, nor for Matthew and Maisie who had come specially to see her. Now she was bright and appreciative, without a jot of conscience for her previous behaviour. We stopped at the door to Mother's lounge. 'In here,' I said. She looked through the door at the lace and Morris-print fabrics of my mother's old maid's room. Then she grabbed my hand and pulled me along the landing.

'Isn't this your room, at the end?' she said, affecting a girlish curiosity.

'No. Please, Nicola . . .' But we were already inside.

I did not want to resist her. She fluffed out her hair and took off her jacket, blouse and skirt. She was wearing the simple white bra and pants I liked. Some thought had gone into this. She smiled by way of explanation. This was her language. For her, words were a secondary form of communication, inadequate. She liked the unspeaking and the most dangerous pleasures. They held no fears for her. What was the point of life, she used to say, if it wasn't to get the things that made you most happy?

'Are you going to stand there all day? Do I have to be naked on my own?'

'Oh, come on, Nicola . . .'

'Be quiet and get undressed.'

She fussed with my trouser belt. I pushed her hand away and did it myself. I really did want her to go, but she knew I could not be so cold-blooded. When I had stripped off she took hold of my head and put her tongue in my mouth. I held her lightly. She had a tendency to heaviness, her breasts large, thighs fleshy and dimpled, spidery veins at the top, though her stomach was firm. Once I had said her figure was

102

classically voluptuous, a description she adored. We went down on the bed. It would be all right, I told myself. We could get back to fighting later. After weeks of self-control I was due a little bad behaviour. And there was the old luxury of not having to think about taking precautions. She seemed to get this message, digging her nails into my back, kissing and licking my face. I entered her and crossed the divide away from my reserve, recovering that lost hot toy of her sex. I rubbed my face over her cold breasts. They smelled of shower gel. I felt the stubble on her calves as she rubbed her legs against mine. We fought against each other for the rhythm. I held back, counting her groans. She was pushing up hard, wanting the world to charge through her, wanting her orgasm, that dearest pleasure of hers. I looked at her face, the half-closed eyes, tendrils of hair in the sweat on her forehead. Missing me, she had said. She was missing me. And at the point of my climax, of her own cries that would be heard as far away as the lobby, Mother listening, leaning on her stick, head cocked to catch the sound, I could almost have believed her.

The brewery delivered at three. I had to be there to open the awkward trapdoor to our tiny cellar about which the draymen always complained, and to give them the order for next week. I left Nicola dozing in bed, her clothes scattered about my boy's-room floor.

The men came at three twenty, lowering the barrels down the cellar ramp with their long ropes. I stood and watched. From the kitchen came a hiss, a clattering pan, Andy's curse, 'Oh, fuck!' Then Lionel drove up to the garage in Mother's car. He had been to the tip with the junk from the storeroom. He got out, smiling.

'I'm sorry, Lionel. I'll come and help in a minute.'

'No worries, old mate. It's sorted. Two trips and that was it.'

'Really, I meant to help.'

'Forget it. Besides, you've got company, haven't you?'

He hung around, watching me, a smugness in his eyes that I found detestable. And when I heard a car start up at the front of the hotel he looked close to laughter, the eyes narrowing under his wiry eyebrows. I went round, under the kitchen windows, arriving in time to see the yellow roof of Nicola's Citroën sliding past the laurels that bordered the drive and the street. I returned to my duties. Lionel was in the kitchen, talking with Andy, his loud laughter rolling through the open door like a drunk being thrown from the premises. I signed the drayman's delivery note, gave him my order, and went round the front of the building and up to my room. On the table was a piece of the hotel's paper with my own pen resting on it. *You're right, Harold. It wouldn't work. I'm sorry. N.*

I sat on my bed, then lay back listening to a gull scratching in the guttering outside. It was a state halfway between wanting to work and needing to rest. A suspension.

16

The clientele of the White Rose taproom was almost exclusively male. They were locals, faces I remembered from my schooldays who now worked as builders, taxi drivers, fare collectors for the mock-up train that ran along the promenade in season. They bore the names of the town's old families; Dent, Wilkinson, Hoggarth, Brolly. I could not consider myself to be one of them. I had been away, seen something of the world. It was my conceited belief that they would not have had such experiences. But really, what did I know? On the scale of fulfilment, that dreamy ladder to the skies of content-ment, had I been more successful than they? I doubted it.

On the day after Nicola had been and gone, I met up with Colin in the Rose, as usual. A school of four was growling in aggressive good humour over the dominoes table, turning the air blue over the laying of a double six. Colin and I were the only others in the room.

Colin drank off his pint. He was drinking faster than usual, determined, troubled. I had spotted as much when I came through the door and saw his face set in consideration of the sticky wooden tabletop. It was a maudlin display, and for my benefit. 'But Harold,' he said again. 'She's thirteen.

Bloody thirteen! It's too young. She's still a girl. They're not as grown-up as they think.'

I wanted to say I didn't know much about this sort of thing, not being a father myself. And I had few gifts for offering the consoling shoulder. But it would have been thoughtless to divert him from the subject. It had him like a fever. 'So, how old is this youth?'

He was standing to go to the bar. He sat down again. 'Eighteen! He's a bloody man, for God's sake. Why can't he find someone his own age? Why does it have to be my daughter?' He was asking himself these things, but needing me as a verbal punch bag. He looked into the empty glass, tilting it against the mat. 'You feel a real failure, Harold. You haven't got kids, you wouldn't know. But I tell you, after all you do for them, everything you tell them, they just turn round and throw it back in your face. They make you feel it's your fault. Like you've driven them to it, for fuck's sake. Ah, it's a bloody life sentence, man. There's no end to it.' He looked across at the men. I imagined him fantasising about hiring a couple of them to sort out this boyfriend, to make a show of old-fashioned morals, the kind of thing Colin had been brought up believing in. I finished my drink and he took both glasses to the bar.

It was hard not to sympathise with Colin. He had lived his life by the book and deserved ordinary luck, if nothing else. As a father he would be a dispenser of convention, his eye for the changing of the world glazed over once he had married, perhaps earlier. Yet was that so bad? The vast majority of society lived by roughly agreed rules. There were laws that stopped us killing each other, but the moral consensus, with its roots in basic religious ethics, was more important. It had to be there. That was how the world kept turning. And yet its generality was everyone's biggest worry – what was right and what we could get away with.

Suddenly, I was thinking of Guy. The thought just popped into my head. Had the protective shield finished its work? Was it time for considered reflection with its attendant little pains? As Colin stood at the bar, jingling the change in his trouser pocket, angry at being ignored by the girl serving in the lounge, I was thinking of Guy, wondering how much of the rest of my life, however decently lived, could count against the horrific act I had been involved in just two months before. My conscience had been off and away, guarded by a wish for self-preservation. I had been dismissing it as a regrettable event, a spot of bother that had to be dealt with outside the boundaries of the law. Maisie was the victim, not Guy. She had made a silly mistake and did not deserve punishment or the humiliation of the courts. Guy was a chancer and had suffered the end of those who strayed too often beyond the boundaries of what was acceptable. The matter of guilt, both mine and Maisie's, need not be on the agenda. It was the way I had been thinking, and the way I wanted things to carry on. But now there was a tinge of culpability to my thoughts. It would pass, I told myself.

Colin came back from the bar. Two men came in and sat near us, looking at the racing page of the evening paper, sharing ideas about the merits of tomorrow's runners, in particular a stayer who, one of them feared, might not get the ground it needed. Colin took no notice of them. He was deep in the mess of his ruminations. I blocked out my thoughts about Guy. We were silent, sitting like bookends, an inviting target for disparaging comments from the boys at their fives and threes. The subject of Colin's daughter was going stale, but at least it was something to talk about. 'What does your wife make of all this?'

'Sheila? Christ! She says girls grow up more quickly than boys. It's a hormonal thing, she reckons, like the way kids are growing so much faster and taller these days. Sometimes I get the feeling she's glad about it all, the way it upsets me. Bloody women! You're best off without them, Harold.'

His aggression put me on edge. 'Well, I have to say it seems a bit heartless. And you're taking a chance, letting them do as they like at that age. Thirteen is very young.'

Colin grinned sourly. 'You're telling me.' He took a sip of his pint, the fifth, a record for one of our weekly meetings. He held the glass in front of him, his stubby corn-trimming fingers firm about its body. He tilted it, looking perplexed by its contents, a muscle dancing in his jaw. 'If he touches her, Harold, if he so much as lays a finger on that girl of mine . . .'

I smiled effetely. 'What?'

He put down the glass, glancing across at the chain-clanking clatter of dominoes, the rapping of knuckles on the board to signal the end of the game. He half turned to me, looking changed, harder, a man resentful of the playground taunts of his boyhood, of the low-value cards he thought life was forever dealing him. 'I'll kill him.'

17

June came blazing, the sky turning the bay an exquisite turquoise against which the yacht club held its red-sailed regatta. And the visitors still came, those people who were meant to have spurned the British holiday resort in favour of EuroDisney, the Canaries, the Far East. Their numbers impressed me. All the town's traders were busy and cheerful. It was an optimism I had forgotten, somewhere between the ages of twelve and fifteen, when I had cultivated a cynicism about what I saw as my parents' limited aspirations. But it kept coming back to me, in brief seconds when nothing seemed to matter any more, when there was just me and the soft coastal breeze and again the sky with its endless blue shading to white on the horizons. While I had been away, living what I thought was my life, there were times when I hated the sea. The screeching of gulls induced a particular mental nausea. I had wanted to deny my childhood and youth. But now I had come full circle and I could accept it all. A salvation of sorts seemed on the cards.

My midlife crisis, if there is such a thing, had been Nicola. The whole two years embodied it. Now I was left with only a lingering fatalism, a hint of the classic breakdown of one's younger self, a surrender of dreams and control. There was a resignation that nothing new was ever going to happen, but with it I sensed a plateau of understanding, a maturity I would look to embrace. In five months I would be forty, but there would be no hysterics from me.

On the first Monday of the month I received a letter from Nicola. She had meant to phone, but did not have the courage. The marriage was over, she knew now. She would not marry again. It was wrong for someone who is so good at hurting people. And I was not to blame myself for our failures. I would not see her again. In fact, she had decided to move to the south of France for a very long time, for as long as it would take to become a decent human being. I read the letter just once. Her fondness for the written word was getting tiresome and I wondered if her last husband, Ken, who she claimed had deserted her after only three months, had suffered this sort of thing, her inability to know her own mind, her fooling around with the expectations of others. Maybe this Ken and I should meet up, form a club of two comparing notes, offering each other advice. And yet Nicola's appearance here had given me a fresh sense of my existence. I felt damaged, and glad to be so. It was a leap forward in the long business of trying to reinvent myself.

I gave Mother a brief explanation that my marriage was now truly dead. It pleased her. And she all but admitted that she had become very used to my being around, loosening her involvement in the running of the hotel. Now she could spend whole afternoons nursing her sore hip in her rooms, emerging only for a light tea and to take her seat at the end of the bar, where she would chat for an hour or two with the guests or Lionel, the pair ruminating about the problem of the local kids meeting on the clifftop for nightly drinking sessions. 'Peg, if they want it, they'll get it. There'll always be somebody ready to sell it to 'em,' Lionel opined, his seriousness contrived for its audience.

On the Friday of that week, Matthew rang. I told him I had kept in touch with Maisie, and tried to talk up her decision to shift universities, making jokey detractions about Newcastle, reassuring him that she seemed happier now. He accepted the explanation, saying Maisie had said much the same thing. But he could not understand why she hadn't discussed it with him first. I waffled through this, saying she was of an age for trying her wings, filling out into adulthood. It did not sound convincing and my brother was quiet for a few moments. Then Mother came and spoke to him.

That afternoon, Mother came down early from her rooms. The call had brightened her, though she was walking with a new rolling movement that made her underclothes rustle, her wrist quivering as she bore weight on the stick. She came into the bar, Kipper trotting in behind her and dropping to his belly on a square of sunlight on the carpet. Mother negotiated her stool with a grimace.

'Is it still hurting?'

'Sometimes.' She twisted closer to the bar. 'Just there.' She felt the small of her back with her palm. 'It's sciatica, I'm sure of it. There's something pressing on the nerve.'

'Can't you take anything for that?'

'I've been trying not to stuff myself with too much medicine. It masks the pain. You don't know if you're doing any real harm.'

She lit a cigarette while I poured her a glass of wine. The first mouthful seemed to revive her and I wondered about her drinking. The old man had been a boozer, particularly in the latter years. And now Mother was doing so little work, she could easily fall into the same trap. But this was a bleary-eyed business, a trade in which one's indulgences passed without comment, habitual excess natural to the territory. For me too, I knew.

'Matthew seemed well,' she said, picking at her nails. 'A bit quiet about Maisie, though. Have you rung her lately?'

'Last weekend. She seems OK. I told him there's nothing to worry about.'

In truth, I had not been able to get hold of her the previous Sunday evening, our usual time. It had bothered me and I had meant to call her during the week. But what if she did not want to speak to me? Maybe she was entering a new phase, coming to terms with what had happened. Or was this a hope of my own? Lately the conversation had been mechanical, Maisie trying to explain the finer details of her course while I prattled about the state of trade, something that had never interested her before.

'She's a strange girl,' said Mother. 'A bit giddy.'

'It's her age. They're not so ready to grow up these days. It's a steadier process. No rush to get married, have kids. And I can't say I blame them.'

'It might be that. Though she does have moods. The last few years in particular.'

I put down the glass I was drying. 'Does she?'

'Oh, ye-es,' she said in that prim way she had when she was imparting new information, correcting someone else's perceptions. 'You weren't here, of course. But Matthew got quite worried.' She looked at the half-smoked cigarette and stubbed it out.

'Worried about what?'

'Well, she'd lock herself in her room for days. Or the school would ring and Matthew would go round and find her sitting on the school steps, still as a statue. He couldn't

112

get through to her. She'd just gaze right through him. Then she'd sleep it off, for a whole day sometimes. It happened a few times, right up to her leaving school.'

Her words alerted me. The dog came and slumped at her feet. 'I didn't know about that.'

'No, well, there seemed no point telling you. She was seeing a psychiatrist for a while, but Matthew didn't want anyone to know. The stigma and all that.'

'The stigma about what?'

'They did these tests, EEG or something. They said it might be a temporary form of epilepsy, but I put it down to the accident, you know, those first few days when she was in the incubator. They thought there might not be enough oxygen getting to the brain. What's it called – deprivation? But there was no way they could test for it. She was too tiny. And then, when she pulled through, we were all ready to accept her for what she was, a lovely healthy baby. It was a miracle. Reg called her the God Child.'

'Yes. Yes, I remember.'

'I never forgot those first few days.' Her look was one of vulgar knowing, a search for my dismay. 'When I look at her, I sometimes think she's still in that incubator thing, just sitting there, looking out at us all.'

'Do you?' I took a cloth and went to wipe the tables, my thoughts taking on an unwanted colouring.

So my niece was more than a victim of adolescent preoccupations. *She had moods.* Had she been telling me the truth about Guy? My conscience took a nasty wrench; the feelings I had evaded for so long seemed to be arriving in all their ugly reality. I ran the cloth over one of the tables, catching my blurred reflection in its copper top. This was unexpected. Had my trust been naive? The story she had told me, that I thought then had been prepared for the police, was it completely true? All I had was her word, and that one glancing meeting in the Trawlerman's. Might Guy have been someone else altogether? A kid from the university? A reasonable lad, with just a bit of a temper? And that night, hadn't Maisie's mood, for all her tears, been rather flat? Then there was the second wound, the scratches. I had been happy to dismiss them. There had been only one true wound. Or had the attack been a more concerted affair?

But it couldn't be so. I knew her well enough. Mother's theory was nonsense, part of her amateur fascination with health matters. I stood looking out of the bay window, at the rockeries and footpaths that led down to the promenade, the kids chasing about the water with their Fun-Tubes, the bathers flat on their towels behind the windbreaks. I was staring. But seeing nothing, failing to convince myself. Until that moment, *I did not think I had done anything wrong*. I pulled myself away from the window and went back behind the bar.

'She likes you,' said Mother.

'What?'

'Maisie. You've been good for her, while Matthew's been away.'

'Have I?'

She was rubbing the back of her neck. 'Yes. It's what Matthew would have wanted.'

I was angry with her, hating her interest in illnesses, anything morbid. The anger came in graded qualities, from the petulance of a schoolboy trying to save face, ready to argue the toss, to the darkest deflation. Why couldn't she have told me about Maisie's moods, these absences? Or why couldn't she have kept this information, if that's what it was, to herself? She was an agent to accusation. I had not needed to know about this. I felt short of air, wanting to be alone, to puzzle out this unforeseen notion.

'It seems an awful long time since Matthew went. I've missed him,' she said. 'And he won't be back till the end of the year, or so he says. Still, it would be nice if he made it for Christmas. And Maisie. We could have a bit of a party. Like the old days.' She looked at me, head to one side. 'If you're still here.'

'I don't know what I'll be doing. I guess I'll still be here, yes.' I was mumbling. Had she been harbouring this question for some time? I could have done without it at that moment.

'Do you mind me asking?'

'No. Of course not. I'm just not sure what my long-term plans might be.'

She nodded slowly. I was hurting her. I couldn't help it, my nerves were fraying. I thought about saying more, making plain my hopes for staying here a good while yet. But the words would not come. I hated her for what she had said about Maisie, the thoughtlessness of it, the way it suddenly threw everything, everything into turmoil. She was a witch, opening her mouth again to compound my misery when Lionel came in behind me.

He took me to one side. 'There's some bloke wants to see you.'

'Is it important?'

Lionel looked at Mother. She was lighting another cigarette. 'I don't know.'

'Well, who is it?'

'He'll tell you.'

I went through to the desk, leaving Lionel with Mother.

The man was wearing a plain brown suit, a blue striped shirt with button-down collar, dust on his tie. He had heavy glasses with brown oyster rims. He was a bloody nuisance, someone from the council, or a rep trying to interest me in the latest line in refrigeration. I would get rid of him quickly, give him short shrift, offload some of my succulent bad temper. He nodded, offering a plastic-covered card across the desk. It bore his photograph, passport-size, a glum younger likeness.

'I'm Detective Constable Pinney, Gateshead CID,' he said. 'I'm investigating a missing-person complaint. Might I take a minute of your time, er, Mr Broome, is it?'

18

'It's a pretty routine matter at the moment. People go
missing every day, by the dozen.' As he spoke, the sentences
were punctuated by a nervy drop of the chin. He took a
leather-covered notepad from his pocket. 'It could well
be nothing. But the family are concerned. I'm sure you'll
understand.'

'Yes. Of course. How can I help?' I straightened the
register and tidied the pens to one side of the desk, actions
to cope with my rushing anxiety.

The policeman smiled, an odd expression, lips stretched
to one side of his face. 'I don't know if you can, actually.
The man we're looking for may have had some kind of a
relationship with a relative of yours, a Maisie Broome.'

The name hit me in the chest. 'She's my niece.'

'Ah, I see.' He hesitated, looking at me. 'We traced her
to Newcastle University. Someone who knows her gave
me her home address. I've been round to the house, but
it seems to be closed up. One of the neighbours told me
you had connections with the family.'

I could not think. It was impossible not to give straight
answers. 'The house belongs to my brother, Matthew,
Maisie's father. He's away in Kuwait. Maisie moved on to
Nottingham, just after Easter. I would have thought they'd

tell you that at the university.' My words were tinged with bad temper. Part of me still thought I was trying to fob off a salesman.

'It was mentioned.' He scribbled on the pad, pausing to squint at the point of his pen. 'But they didn't tell me much. Some code of confidentiality they have. Why did she leave?'

'I'm not really sure. She wasn't very happy there, you know, in digs, first time away from home. Is it important?'

'Maybe not. We don't know yet. Look . . .' From his inside jacket pocket he produced a photograph. 'This is the chap. Have you seen him before, Mr Broome?'

I took the picture, holding it tightly between thumb and forefinger to stop my hand from shaking. It was Guy, sitting in a pub behind a table stacked with glasses, balloons, Christmas streamers. He was laughing, flushed scarlet, holding up a pint pot. Not a decent lad. A bum. I made a show of concentrating, scratching my cheek while I studied, looking to the left of Guy's face for a few seconds, unable to stomach its known expression. 'I'm sorry. He doesn't look familiar. Perhaps if I checked the register. What's his name?'

'Winterton.' The chin went forward and back. 'Guy Winterton.' He did not seem interested in my offer to look through the register. 'He was known to wear a distinctive red overshirt thing. It had a motif on the back that said "DO IT" or something.'

I shook my head, though the details were destroying me by the second. 'I'm sorry . . .'

The boom of Lionel's laughter came from the bar. Pinney looked towards the open door, and back to me. 'Mr Broome, does your niece have many boyfriends?'

I shrugged, handing him back the photograph. 'I wouldn't know. I imagine there's been an admirer or two. She's an attractive girl.'

He put the photograph on the desk while he wrote, Guy looking up at me, red face frozen in crass celebration. 'There was no one here with her earlier in the year?'

'No, I don't remember anyone. I didn't see much of her, to be honest. I'm not the sort of company she would keep socially. Too old, you know?' I grinned. There were vapours of sweat above my top lip.

Pinney smiled, seeming to appreciate the comment. He made a quick note, a squiggle that could have been no more than three words. 'You say her father's in Kuwait?'

'Yes.'

'Her mother?'

'She's dead.' He looked up, mouth open to invite elaboration. I could see the yellow tongue of a smoker. 'A car accident. A long time ago.' There was no reason to give every detail, to panic, to relay so instantly Mother's ponderings on Maisie's state of mind. My confidence was growing.

'Right.' He finished writing, looking about the lobby, towards the staircase, as if he was trying to remember something. He folded over the pad and put it in his pocket. 'Well, I'd rather like to see your niece, Mr Broome.'

'I'm sure she'll be only too pleased to help,' I said, but my assurance was too abrupt, drawing a sidelong glance from behind the thick glasses. In my anxiety, I wanted to add to the comment, saying that my niece was an obliging sort, but I managed to keep my silence. Two of our guests came in. I followed their path to the bar, where Lionel's voice was again echoing in the doorway. I wanted to give the impression of being a busy man who needed to be about his business.

'Mmm. Nottingham. What's that, about a hundred miles or so from here?'

'About that. If you aim for the Humber Bridge.'

'Oh, right.' He smiled. 'Actually, the reason I ask is that it might be an overnight job, and I don't know if the force's budget will run to that kind of expense. I'd have to ask first. Stupid, isn't it? Everything's to do with money these days.' I did not know what to make of this. The informality seemed deliberate.

'Surely, if the family are worried?'

'Yes. You'd think that would matter, wouldn't you? Thing is, this lad . . .' He picked up the photograph and frowned at it. 'He's not the most wholesome character. Known to us, you could say. And the last time anyone saw him, he'd been stinking drunk for days. Then he just took off. Not a word to anyone.' He put the photograph back in his pocket. 'He could be anywhere, really. It's what he's like, a drifter. And one day, likely as not, he'll just turn up on his mother's doorstep. A typical Geordie lad. They all come back when they want feeding. Can you tell me which college your niece is at?'

'Yes, I have the name somewhere. If you'll excuse me a second.'

I went into the office, half closing the door, glad of the chance to breathe freely. I screwed up my eyes, made fists with my hands. I opened a desk drawer and closed it again. Too much hesitation might look suspicious. So might too great a keenness to help. I had to appear averagely, politely concerned. The name of Maisie's college, and her phone number, were on a scrap of paper on the notice board. I knew them off by heart, but still looked up at the board to copy down the address. I went back to the policeman. 'Here. I have her phone number as well, somewhere, if you want to ring her first.'

'Probably not. I'll just find her for myself. Who knows,' he said, 'I might bump into Winterton on my way down there. Stranger things have happened at sea. And it'd save an awful lot of trouble.' He put my note in his pocket and extended his hand. 'Thank you for your time, Mr Broome.'

He was going, but I did not want him to. The worry he would leave me with would be too great. I wanted both mine and Maisie's innocence made irrefutably clear. And now. I had handled this badly. Later, I would think of the million and one things I might have said to outwit this man. I shook his hand, trying to look him up and down. He was about thirty, the brown hair a bit greasy. The spectacles were the thing to remember, the main detail I would need to tell Maisie about, since I was very certain I would have to get hold of her before he did.

'I'm sorry I couldn't be more help,' I said. He smiled. He had overlapping front teeth.

As I went round the desk to walk to the door with him, Mother appeared from the bar, taking Kipper out for his afternoon run in the garden. Pinney watched her, his eyes brightening. Should I introduce them? Mother nodded as she passed, making her slow way across the carpet to the kitchen. When she was through the door, Pinney was still looking, smiling.

'Do you know, I have some really fond memories of this town. We used to come here on holiday when I was a lad.'

I did not believe this. He was still fishing, looking for bits of my character, my honesty. 'A great many people "used to" come here,' I said, with all

121

the friendliness I could muster. 'Not so many these days.'

'That's a shame. It's a nice place. Quiet. The people are nice. Is the lifeboat house still here?'

'It went some time ago.'

'Now that is sad. Still, I might go and have a look down on the prom. For old times' sake.' He paused, as if chewing over this idea. Now I had seen enough of him. I wanted him to go. He nodded to some thought of his own. 'Thank you again for your trouble, Mr Broome.'

'As I said, I'm sorry I couldn't help you more. If I think of anything, I'll let you know.' This was the first betrayal of my nerves. Where would I get in touch with him? I was losing my grip. If he stayed another ten minutes I would crack and confess all. He might already have sensed this, his experience alerted to the smell of fear, the electricity it produced in a suspect.

He headed for the door, stopping to tap the barometer. 'Set for change,' he said.

'It's always set for change.'

'Yes.' He looked back towards the desk. 'Right. Well, goodbye, Mr Broome.'

'Cheerio.'

He walked slowly down the drive to the street, looking both ways as if unsure where he should begin the pursuit of his stupid childhood memories. He crossed the road to a red Sierra parked outside the baker's shop, a breeze lifting the flap of his jacket. He nodded to a tourist, got in the car and drove off in the opposite direction to the beach, glancing up at the Finlandia as he passed.

I leaned against the wall, drained. Mother reappeared from the kitchen. 'And who was that?'

'I don't know,' I snapped. 'He was looking for someone. I couldn't help him.'

'Who was he looking for?'

'I said I don't know, didn't I?'

I went round the desk and into the office, closing the door behind me.

19

My palms were damp. Somehow I had to calm down. I took the whisky from the drawer and poured a drink, thinking back to the earlier part of the day, my equability of not fifty minutes before. It was a mockery now. I took a drink, the gesture alone making me feel better. But the urgency of the situation was horribly pressing. Where else might this Pinney go in Oughton? There was the Trawlerman's, though the staff did not know me there and incidents such as Guy and Maisie's outburst went on at the pub every Friday night. Worse, usually. Then there were the Charltons, the old sisters along the row from Matthew's house. I did not really know them, yet suddenly I saw them as English citizens of a bygone age, happy to fulfil a lifelong wish to help the police with their enquiries, confusing the picture with wittery, unreliable embellishments. Then there were the people opposite, families who might have lived there for ten years, for all I knew. Someone had told Pinney of the connection between the house and the Finlandia. How nosy were they, damn them? What might they have remembered of the day Guy arrived in Oughton? Was this detective, or whatever he was, closer to the truth than he had let on? Much closer? It was impossible to know. I would have to take him on face value and believe that so far he knew little. I finished the drink, needing a minute or two to move around and let my thoughts settle before I rang Maisie to warn her. I went into the bar.

Lionel was lolling on the pumps, shirt-sleeved, chatting with a man he seemed to know. He stood up as I entered. 'Has he gone?' He was smiling.

'Yes. He was trying to find someone. Couldn't help him.' I was slurring the words, not because of the whisky, just my nerves afloat.

'Well, don't worry!' Although wrapped in condescension, it felt like sympathy, and I was glad of it. Don't worry – the words on their own had a glancingly soothing effect. For a tiny moment, in my confusion, I liked Lionel. He was a friend to the family. 'I'm all right here,' he said. 'If you want to take a break.'

The offer could not be refused, despite the suspicion it might arouse. 'Yes. I think I might.'

I went back through the lobby and up the stairs. The whisky had dulled my predicament. I had an inclination to get drunk, to let the police do what they would . . . But that would not do. Climbing the last narrow flight to the top floor, I resolved to objectify the situation. It was a project I was involved in, like a an urgent business deal. I went into Mother's lounge and sat on the sofa with its heap of chintzy cushions, the telephone on a glass-topped bamboo table at my side. On the mantelpiece was a picture of Matthew at thirteen and myself aged ten, a posed portrait with our cheeks freshly scrubbed, not a hair out of place. Next to this was a photograph of the old man in his blazer and flannels, raising his pipe aloft as if about to make one of his half-baked analyses of life, the universe, or the kind of soil best for hydrangea. And in the corner, beside the chimney breast, was Mother's portrait of Maisie, fourteen years old, dramatic red flecks in the straw hair, a blue and purple lividness in the complexion. It was actually rather good, an almost worrying representation, the eyes probing the middle distance, my niece pensive, melancholy. What had Mother been thinking about when she painted the thing? Her theory about Maisie's moments of distraction?

The room was bathed in sunlight, the heat loosening the old-woman's fustiness from the carpet and the lace-covered furniture. I did not know what I was going to say to Maisie. It would be a pragmatic thing. But first I had to get organised. I put the phone in my lap and rang Colin, for the first time in my life, to say I would not be out that night. He accepted with unexpected good humour, as if my ringing him been a new sign of our developing friendship. Then I rang Maisie, concentrating on the flowery hearth rug, avoiding the look of the pictures around me.

A young man answered. 'She's not here right now.' There was a television on in the background.

'Do you know when she'll be back?'

'Couldn't say, really.'

'Well, will she be in a lecture?'

'It's possible.' His tone was maddeningly indifferent. How moronic young people were, how self-centred, ignorant of detail. He covered the mouthpiece and I heard him mumble to someone nearby. He took his hand away. 'She's been out since this morning. About eleven.'

'Right. Could you get her to ring me the moment she comes in?'

'Sure. I'll leave a note,' he said, seeming more alert. 'Who is it?'

'Just tell her Harold called.'

'And it's urgent, is it?'

'Yes. Tell her I need a word with her as soon as possible.'

I put down the phone without saying goodbye. I looked at my watch: a quarter to six. I would give it another twenty minutes and ring again. I went downstairs.

The lobby was full of people with suitcases and folded summer coats. Lionel was at the desk despatching keys. It was a party from a British Legion club in Leeds, here for the weekend. I cursed. I had forgotten about them completely. Even Mother was helping out, standing at the side of the desk, telling an old woman where she would find her room, explaining with her practised regret that we had no lift. And how she wished, with her bad hip, that there was one!

For a moment, I could not face this extra activity. I went through to the kitchen. Andy had not yet arrived for his evening stint. I wanted another drink, the first taste chasing the next. But there would be nothing in here, save for the cheap sherry for the trifles. I headed for the cupboard where it was kept, then stopped myself. This was foolish. I must not allow myself to get drunk. I could hear the chatter and banter in the lobby. Lionel was certain to have spotted me coming in here. I had to get back to work. For the benefit of anyone who might be watching through the open door, I drank a glass of water and returned to the lobby. Most of the dozen or so new arrivals had either gone to their rooms or were in the bar.

'Little flurry there, Harold,' Lionel said. 'It's the darts-team outing. Third year running. We could be up late tonight.' He grinned. 'If the last two years are anything to go by.'

'I'd better see to the bar,' I said.

'Good idea. You're learnin'.'

Mother was already at her seat, giving me a careful look

as I began pulling pints, mixing snowballs and martinis. I did not want this. It would have been better to be alone, to nurture my worry. I kept checking my watch discreetly, every minute, trying to gauge how long it would take Pinney to get to Nottingham. Two hours, perhaps longer with the teatime traffic.

It was seven o'clock before I could slip away to the office to ring Maisie again. This time a girl answered. Maisie had still not returned. She was more sympathetic than the boy I had spoken to and I regretted my earlier feelings about young people. She rattled off a list of friends' flats, pubs, places where my niece might be, but confessed to not really knowing where she might have gone. I put the phone down. The guests who had gone straight to their rooms were reappearing outside the closed door, heading for the bar to join their friends. The temptation was to ring again, immediately, the process of making this call suddenly addictive. It would have been better if there had been no one in the house where Maisie was staying. I could ring every minute, relishing the anticipation of hearing Maisie's voice. I looked at the clock on the wall. Two seconds became a long time, the second hand taking an eternity to break for the tick, eventually moving, then snagging before its grudging progress to the next mark. I strove to be rational. To call again in half an hour would be reasonable. The kids she was sharing the house with would be used to anxious relatives on the phone: the father concerned over his daughter's virginity, the mother who had heard so much about drugs and young people. Thirty minutes. I measured the distance the minute hand would have to travel before I tried again, and went back to the bar.

The new arrivals were in loathsome high spirits. They

shouted their orders, tipped over glasses, competed to see who were enjoying themselves the most. 'Thees' and 'thars' flooded the talk, a repulsive reminder of where I was, where I had ended up in life – a hard nowhere. The floorboards were creaking above my head as some of their number were finding their way about the rooms, then, halfway through a request for seven different drinks, the phone rang in the office. I shot through. But it was only someone who had stayed earlier in the week, asking if we had found a cardigan in her room. The disappointment was not too great. At least the phone had rung. Somehow it might make the line warm, inviting Maisie to get hold of me.

In the bar, I finished serving the round. The man paying offered to buy me a drink and, against hotel policy, I accepted, Mother was watching. I was taking drinks, I was not wearing the stupid white jacket. What the fuck. I took a measure of scotch, drank it, and put the glass up to the optic for another.

By eight thirty the bar had emptied down to the usual three or four dotted about the room. The darts team had gone to the affiliated club in Ash Street. I felt drunk and resigned. What was the point in ringing again? If Maisie had been in she would have called immediately. I refuted Mother's ideas about her granddaughter's state of mind. Maisie was all right. She was a good girl. There was nothing wrong with her. I knew this, for the comfort it afforded.

'Are you all right, Harold?' Mother was watching me from her seat.

The room was littered with the darts team's debris. I should go and clear it up, a job I quite liked, the restoring of order. I made a move to begin, but wobbled on my feet. I would have to stay where I was until my head cleared a little. 'I'm fine. Why?'

'You seem a bit agitated, that's all.'

'I'm not. A bit tired, maybe. I haven't eaten since lunch.'

'Why don't you go and get something?'

'I don't know where Lionel is.'

'Don't worry. He'll be about. I'll call if I can't manage.'

I was standing with one hand on the shelf behind me, unable to hide my drunken air, this state of abstraction. 'All right. I'll be in the office.'

The drink had been a mistake. It was letting me down. I sat in the office and rubbed my eyes. I could have done with a wash. The phone was silent on the desk. Eight forty-five. Pinney would be in Nottingham, if he had gone that evening. Perhaps I had been too keen on this idea and he had gone back north to resume his enquiries after the weekend? Part of me no longer wanted to be bothered with this whole affair. The struggle between hope and indifference was overwhelming me. My life was in chaos and I was too tired, too unfit for it all. Yet there was no way out, no rest for my beating heart. That was the worst part. I took the scotch from the drawer and poured a kamikaze measure. It would oil the depression, transform it into mere resignation. I took a sip, and the phone rang.

'Harold?'

It was Maisie. In an instant, my energy returned.

'Maisie? Look, I've been trying to ring you. Is there anyone there?'

'No.'

'Well, listen. There's a man coming to find you,' I said, keeping my voice firm and steady. 'His name's Pinney. He's from the police – '

'I know. I've already seen him.'

'What?'

130

'Half an hour ago. He found me in the college café. I was there with some friends.'

'Shit.' I whispered the word to myself. 'What did he say?'

'He just wanted to know if I'd seen Guy lately.'

'And?'

'I said he'd been down to Oughton before Easter. What else could I say? People saw us together. We were in the pub. There was your friend there, that chiropodist,' she said, her voice cracking. 'Uncle Harold, I'm scared. I'm fed up with it all.'

I waited a few seconds, realising this was the first time we had mentioned Guy in months. Our calls to each other had all been exercises in cheerfulness, skirting round this huge subject I never saw fit to mention. That could not be helped now. 'So you said you saw Guy. You met up. Then what?'

She gave a little groan. 'I feel like giving myself up. I can't live with all this . . .'

'Maisie, love. Just keep your head a minute. What else did you tell Pinney?'

'I said Guy had been drunk. We had a row and he cleared off.'

'Where did you say he'd gone?'

'I said I didn't know. I said he'd been planning to go to Greece. Either that or he'd gone back home.'

Greece! The word was exciting, a new possibility for misleading Pinney, swirling in the complications of the moment. 'And how did he take that?

She sighed. 'I don't know. He seemed sort of satisfied. He knew about the Greece thing. And I got the impression he thought Guy was a pain anyway, a waste of his time.'

131

'But that's good, Maisie. Very good. Where's Pinney now?'

'On his way back to Newcastle, I suppose. He didn't say.'

I pushed the whisky across the desk. I did not need it just now. My black mood had gone. Greece, of course. This could be working out unbelievably well. In the lobby, Lionel was talking and laughing with someone, leading them to the front door. I curled around the phone, keeping my voice low. 'Maisie, I want you to listen very carefully – '

'Harold, I'm frightened. Sometimes I just feel so awful. I cry and cry . . .'

I was getting impatient with her. 'Well, don't. It's not that bad.'

'Not for you, maybe. I can't help it. I want someone to talk to. All the words build up and up and I can't let them out.' She was crying. I wondered if there was anyone in the room with her.

In my elation, I had been expecting too much from her. She was still a child, vulnerable to conscience. I would have to do more to help and coerce, to get her mind thinking properly. 'I'll come down and see you.'

'There's no need for that.'

'You're upset. I think there's every need. I'll come tomorrow,' I said, an impetuous offer.

'But it's the weekend, your busy time.'

'They can manage without me. I'll offer Lionel overtime. He always needs the money.'

'What'll you tell Gran?' The voice was squeaky again.

'Don't worry. I'll think of something.'

'It'll be another lie. It's all lies these days.'

'No, it's not. Look, I'll drive down and meet you at that square in the middle of town – what's it called?'

'Where the market is?'

'That's it. Can you meet me there, say three o'clock?' There was a silence. 'Maisie?'

I could hear her breathing. She sighed. 'Yes. All right.' And put down the phone.

20

So what did I really know of my niece, her life?

Three months after the accident, Matthew goes to work at a college in Scarborough. Maisie is round at the hotel much of the time, a tiny thing, dominating. I know so little about children, babies. It is soon after that I leave, travelling south to look for work, to make some vague point about finding a new life. It has nothing to do with Maisie, I swear.

Maybe I spend too much time nurturing my own interests, guarding my comforts, small though they now seem.

I remember her at nine or ten years old, reading a poem she has been selected to write to commemorate the opening of her school's swimming pool. She is tall for her age, a spindle-legged doll, hair in bunches, reading too quickly. Mother is watching, mouthing the words after Maisie has read them. Matthew is there too, in a bulky jumper with a checked shirt underneath. From him there is a cooler regard, a wince at mistakes. She finishes to applause from the gathered parents and the town's councillors with their forced interest. Matthew nods his approval and later, on the wet winter grass, they shake hands. It is how they are, friends to each other.

At what age has Maisie realised she is motherless? How

easily has she accepted this? Yet for all its drawbacks, she is a happy, rounded child. Matthew's devotion does him credit. It is the family way, not sentimental, not designed, but friendly, born of humour.

And I am away again, seeing her only at odd intervals, startled by the process of growing, marking her progress at yearly intervals when I make my dutiful, dreary trips home to see the family. Each time her changes shock me. I measure them against my own life, which seems so static in comparison. Soon she will catch me up, be adult, successful, supersede me. It is of no concern. She was a miracle baby. Her life is starred for memorable achievement.

At fifteen no doubt she is on the clifftop with the other kids, wondering about that odd look in the boys' eyes and trying the booze for size. It is nothing new. Matthew did it. And I did it too, sneaking bottles from the Finlandia bar, selling them to the others at twenty pence a time. It has always gone on. My brother would know, and I imagine his wisdom in dealing with it unfussily. He would say, 'There's just the two of us. Don't let me down.' And it would be enough. For Maisie is a good girl. It is a truth. For all my avuncular failures, I know it, recognising my own blood in her. We are a decent lot. Known for it . . .

My excuse to Mother was that my solicitor had come up with a scheme, tied in with the divorce settlement, to get me absolved from bankruptcy. We had arranged to meet in Sheffield. It was an overnight job. We were old friends. It was improbable – the house Nicola and I had bought, our one asset, was unsaleable – though Mother accepted it surprisingly well. Maybe she knew it was too elaborate a tale, one of the complications of my past life she saw fit not to question, provided I stayed with her. Even so, I hated lying. As I got older, the deceits seemed to come with less facility. And lately there had been so many, piling up, a teeming heap of dishonesty by which I sat with my smiles, avoiding the business of guilt. I would fantasise about atoning for all this at a later, convenient date, perhaps through some dramatic or charitable act: the dash into a burning house to save a child, the rescue of an old people's home funded by a stroke of good fortune in my finances. None of this would happen, of course. It never did, not in an ordinary lifetime.

Despite the difficulty of the day and evening that lay ahead of me, my spirits lifted of their own accord, at some quick point beyond the town's boundaries and the sign that said, *Come Back Soon for a Real Oughton Bay Welcome.* If nothing else, it was good to get away. When I thought of what lay ahead, my conscience came back in the way I had always predicted – a slight discomfort to the side of me, in the passenger seat. I took no notice, crimping my mouth, listening to the rumble of the unbalanced front wheels, chattering to myself that the car had probably not made such a long journey since the old man had died. My nerve felt good and I was over the shock of Pinney's appearance at the Finlandia. After a night's sleep, the fact of it became manageable and I was happy to believe he was not too keen on following the trail. It could even be useful. Officialdom had taken an interest and found nothing. The affair could go no further. It was an optimism I was keen to impress Maisie with.

I was in Nottingham at a quarter to three. I parked the car, put my bag on my shoulder and headed straight for the Old Market Square. I wanted the process of waiting, something I had always enjoyed, the anticipation, the forced idleness. But after a few minutes among the crowds I was edgy. Perhaps Maisie would not turn up? She might have lost her wits and got in touch with Pinney. Maybe one of the 'absences' that Mother had told me about had come over her. And what was I to make of that anyway? I paced among the pigeons with this unease, risking half-minutes in the side streets, watching people browsing outside shoe shops, newspaper sellers, gangs of cherry-faced, laughing men on their way to the next pub. I resisted the urge to have a drink myself. Later, certainly. But not now. This was a pressing matter. And then she came, drawing the furtive glances of passing husbands, her hair loose on a denim jacket, my own blood, a miracle baby. The God Child.

I gave her a hug, wanting to hold her longer, for the touch to make a statement of my loyalty. 'It's good to see you. Really good. Are you OK?'

She smiled. 'So-so.'

It was an uneasy moment. We were strangers to each other. In our dozen or so telephone conversations, we had not come to know each other any better. I shuffled the bag up on my shoulder. 'Come on, there's a pub I've seen. I want to book in there, then you can tell me what you get up to round here.'

'Are you staying the night?'

'Yes.'

'Oh, God.' She laughed nervously, taking a step back. 'I thought you'd just be here a few hours.'

'Why? Have you got something on?'

'No, no.' 'She was smiling, with her head to one side.

I gave her a teasing look. 'I can go, if you like.'

She smiled. 'No. It's good that you can stay. I'm pleased.'

'That's all right, then.' I put my hand on her shoulder and looked for the street where I had seen the pub.

*   *   *

137

In the room she sat on the bed and watched me unpack my few bits and pieces. It was an intense sort of watching, like the fascination with which, as a toddler, she used to trail my father as he worked in the kitchen. I sensed an advantage in this, making my movements deliberate and visible.

An hour later, we were in a cheap Italian restaurant, a favoured venue for students. We talked about her, exclusively, about her studies, the house she was sharing a mile out of town. She chirruped about her friends, saying how much nicer they were than the people she had known in Newcastle. How they had to be. This last point was offered light-heartedly, then she gave a little gasp, licking her lip with the tip of her tongue. She went quiet. We were getting close to the point. To mention Guy's name could be brutal, but it would have to come up some time. She put down her fork and rubbed her eyes. A woman was watching from the next table.

'Is the meal all right?' I asked.

Maisie nodded, wiping her lips with her finger. 'It's fine. Thanks.' The skin around her eyes was pink. I looked at the woman and she turned away. Maisie put her napkin on the table. Her head drooped with two definable nods. 'Actually, I think I've had enough.'

'OK. We could go back to the pub, if you like.'

'No. Maybe later.'

I paid the bill and we walked the streets for a while, gravitating with tacit consent towards the town centre. We walked in silence, my look drawn by shop-window displays, my head heavy with all we had yet to say to each other. I suggested a drink, but Maisie said she hardly drank at all these days. The sky was dull, the light fading early, and the longer we stayed off the subject of Pinney and Guy, the more difficult it was to approach. We walked towards the castle like tired tourists, the high spirits of the crowds outside the Trip to Jerusalem an affront to my sobriety. Then at a small park, we stopped and sat down on a bench. Across the grass a man was turning off the lights in the public toilets. To my right were office blocks and a main road feeding traffic into town. 'We've a lot to talk about, Maisie.'

She looked to the sky, her expression one of ungainly suffering, tainting her good looks. 'I know. There's no getting away from it, is there?'

'Tell me what Pinney said to you.'

She bit her top lip, blinking slowly. 'I couldn't figure him out. He seemed a bit of a creep. A bit oily, like you just couldn't trust him. Yet he was no problem, really. He even bought me a drink.'

This sounded encouraging, the copper fancying his chances with a young girl, indifferent to his case. 'You said you were with some friends when he found you. Did he talk to you in front of them?'

'I sat in a corner with him. It was weird. I was so shocked by him just turning up like that, it made me feel, I don't know, almost as if I didn't care what he was going to do to me. Suddenly that's what I thought. It didn't seem to matter, one way or the other. It would be a relief to get it over with.'

The man finished locking the toilets and looked our way, dropping his keys in his overall pocket. 'So what did he say?'

'Like I said on the phone, I just got the impression that he thought it was all a waste of his time. He'd had a load of hassle from Guy's family. Or maybe he wanted me to think that way?'

The weight of what we had done lay all around us, a horrible crush that made me silent. There was no escaping it.

The beep of a pedestrian crossing sounded along the road. A rap beat came from the open window of a waiting car. I would have to speak, to push out the words. 'I know what you mean. Well, I thought he was a bit cagey too. But if you think about it, Maisie, if we don't hear from him, that would be that. Case closed. Nothing else to worry about.'

The traffic resumed its speedy momentum into town. Maisie sat forward. 'It would be nice if it was that easy.'

I squeezed her arm. 'It can be. Why shouldn't it be?'

'I don't know. I think about him.' She sat back again.

'Who? Pinney?'

'No.' She rubbed her head, looking down at the grass. 'Guy. I think about him when it gets dark. In the daylight I seem able to forget it all. Life's going on, people are doing things. I've got things to do. It just slips from my mind.'

'Isn't that a good thing?'

She shook her head. 'I don't know. It doesn't last. After a while I feel bad about not remembering, not banging myself over the head with it. And then I do remember, when it's getting dark and people are winding down and I want to yell at them to keep going, keep working. But they don't. That's when it really gets to me. Maybe I'm just frightened of being alone.'

A breeze ruffled clumps of fading broom beyond the railings opposite. The toilet man disappeared. Two women came by with kids in pushchairs, shooing the pigeons off the path. I looked at Maisie, watching for any sign of aberration. But she was just as I had always known her, had always imagined her to be. Mother had made

140

an unforgivable presumption. There was nothing wrong with Maisie. The women passed. Maisie lit a cigarette and nibbled her nails. 'What worries you most?' I asked.

She tutted. 'The guilt. Thinking about him just lying . . . wherever. Everything, really. It's a big horrible lump in my head. Black and horrible, never getting any smaller.'

'Would it help if I said you had nothing to reproach yourself for?'

She blew smoke in her lap. 'I tell myself that. But I don't know . . .' She swept her hair back, a serious gesture. 'He was a human being, he had a right to life the same as anyone.'

'He was an animal.'

'How do you know that? How can you be so sure? All right, he was a shit. But there must have been some good in him. There's good in everyone if you give them the chance to show it.' It was a wisdom I had not expected, a Christianity that made me feel callous.

'There wasn't much goodness in his dealings with you.'

Maisie winced and shook her head. 'I want to forget all that, really I do.'

'Then do it. Just let go.'

'I can't. It's not right.'

'What's not right?'

'This . . . all this carry-on.' She threw away the cigarette and put her hands between her knees. 'Harold, we should have gone to the police. It might've been all over by now. I could have got self-defence. I could have started a new life. Anywhere.'

'You have a new life. This is it. It can't be that bad.' I wanted to say that this had been the better option, that there was no turning back anyway, but it would have been too blunt. 'You shouldn't give yourself such a hard time.'

'I can't help it. I mean, even if nothing ever comes of all this, I'll still feel it's a wrong I can never put right. And what if Dad ever found out? It'd kill him.'

'He'll never know. It's our secret, mine and yours. And we can help each other get over it. Believe me.' The argument was becoming circular, a raking-about in Maisie's muddy feelings. I was getting impatient. It was time to stop placating her, to press further, to extract a promise from her that she would not do anything rash without telling me first. She could sort out her feelings later.

'He keeps sending me cheques. I wish he wouldn't. I'd saved enough before I came here. I cash them, but I won't spend it.' She put her hand on my knee and smiled. 'You're just like him, you know. You're so nice, Harold.'

The comment took me unawares, as if I had needed someone to say that to me. Then three boys came into the park, chasing about the grass, spraying each other with cans of lager. The toilet man appeared, rattling his keys, giving them a measured look. One of the boys drop-kicked an empty can over the railings in reply, and they trooped away with a lolloping tread. It was time to go. The promise I wanted from Maisie would have to wait. 'Come on, I'll see you back to your house. You can introduce me to your friends.'

'Are you sure?' she said, surprised.

'Of course. I need to know they're looking after you properly.'

She gestured theatrically. 'Meet – Uncle Harold!' She laughed.

'Yes.' I was pleased that she was brightening. 'Your old decrepit Uncle Harold.'

We walked out to the road, looking for a taxi.

21

Maisie saw me off the next day. She was glad I had met her new friends, a more likable bunch than I had imagined. I stayed up with them until two in the morning, drinking canned beer, wanting something stronger to flatten the slight headache I was feeling.

I had no chance to make Maisie give me her word that she would not do anything on impulse, but the rest of my effort seemed worth it and I drove back to Oughton certain that I had eased some of the pressure on her. Yet over the next few days, with no further word from Pinney, it began to seem too easy. I felt a niggling unrest, as if in taking away Maisie's pain I was now carrying it myself, in odd pockets of the mind. Her innocent trust in the righteousness of the law, which I had dismissed as naive, kept coming back to me, showing me up, baring an inclemency I did not think I possessed. I tried to ignore it, but during idle moments it came creeping back, a taintedness looking for air.

One evening I was watching Kipper on the floor of the empty bar. He was lying with his back to me, chewing a hide bone. There was something about the way he sprawled, the head bobbing, the lift of one shoulder, his leg crooked like an elbow, that shook me. In a few startling moments he was taking on human characteristics. More specifically I had the impression – as if the dog had acquired this from a lifetime in human company – of a lolling adolescent male, like one of Maisie's student friends.

Like Guy.

I stayed looking, trying to exorcise the demon in my head, this brushing wing of insanity. In my youth I had experimented with LSD at a friend's house, listening to Pink Floyd, watching moving patterns on the carpet, giggling insanely over nothing. The experience bored me and I never bothered again. But I had read of people experiencing flashbacks, ten, fifteen years later. Was that happening to me as I watched the dog roll on his back, toss the bone aside, shake himself and run from the room? The phase passed. I put it down to unrelieved tension.

The days went by with no further word from Pinney. I took to checking the newspapers again, finding nothing. Maybe it was all over. There was a distance of more than three months between me and the event. It would be enough, surely. I felt I should guard against complacency, but there was nothing to get uptight about, nothing I could do. And I was tired of worry, of the whole business concerning Guy. Now I could go for days without thinking about what had happened. It seemed I was forgetting at last. But the memory keeps a dispassionate record. You live your life, go about your dealings with people, but so much remains inside, ineradicable.

Two weeks after I had seen Maisie I woke in a filthy sweat, chest tight as if my heart had been working dangerously hard. A bad dream. First I had been shovelling earth into a hole in the garden behind the Finlandia. Next I was in the hole, having the soil pushed on top of me in some maniacally funny game. There was no recognisable pattern to the dream, but it seemed to slip a gear and Guy was in the hole next to me. He was giggling, telling me it wasn't so bad. I could not feel the soil on top of me, but I could see it, as if I was under a sheet of glass and the earth was falling on that, blocking the sky. I felt for Guy's hand, saying it was time we got out of there. But he had gone.

I looked at my watch on the bedside chair. Five thirty. It was already light, the sun up over the sea, beating hard on this side of the hotel. I lay back. It was not the first time I had dreamed about Guy, though the earlier episodes had been fragmentary with him making cameo appearances, sometimes as a much younger boy. On other occasions I would wake remembering only a vague man, an amalgam of modern youth with its dress and loud manner, that could have been anyone. But that particular morning the fading face was undoubtedly Guy's.

Waking early troubled me. It was, I had read, a complaint of early middle age. It was the subconscious getting restless, overloaded. Too much stress.

I looked about the room, that same room I had grown up in, slept in with my little fears about school, about the noises made by the hotel's tired old plumbing. In those days the wallpaper had a pattern of tiny rockets and planets with cartoon spacemen sitting on top. I used to wonder how they were meant to live in such a small area. It was illogical. They could walk round it in seconds. Where did they get food, water? Where was the toilet, the television? Where would they sleep? The room had been redecorated at least three times since then, yet the ghost of those days lived on behind the new glossed Anaglypta. It was still my room, restricting, a comment on my failure to make out in life. But I was only thirty-nine. It was not too late to start again. And the peace I had imagined finding here, the quiet dissembling into middle age, suddenly struck me as

145

morbid. It may have been the dream that rattled me, but I found myself thinking that come October and the end of the busy season, I should get away again. I still had contacts at two London clubs. With a little effort, surely I could find something? You don't need much of a CV in my game, a year here, six months there, bar people are all the same. Mother would be disappointed, though she must understand that I had my life to lead, that there was still time for me to become someone new, someone innocent.

Throughout that day, the possibility of leaving grew to a near certainty. I was rediscovering myself, a natural confidence it had been perverse to forget. The impulse to leave became irresistible and I revised the date of my departure hourly, checking the hotel's advance bookings, joyfully noting that September was almost empty. Indeed, why wait that long? There was only Mother to consider, and a few raised eyebrows from Lionel and the rest of the staff. And if I did not have to hear their giggling on the landings about the restless son who could not settle to anything, I need not care.

The hot morning gave way to a bright, windy coolness, a symptom of the coast's mercurial climate. You could walk along the promenade and pass from one weather front to another in the space of fifty yards, the sea turning brown and ruffled, the tarmac still hot as the hail rattled down. Had this something to do with my brittle temperament, the wilfulness of the weather having seeped into my bones as a child? Maybe not. It was a fancy idea, but that day I was given to a more concrete way of thinking.

Six of the Finlandia's rooms were occupied. The bar was busy throughout the day, something I enjoyed, the movement of people, the buzz of business always having thrilled me to some degree. That was something from my childhood – my father's animation when things were going well, flitting around the place in his white shirt and gold satin cravat, wafting cheap aftershave in his wake. He loved the idea of success, wanting to capitalise endlessly on any small rush of activity. It affected both Matthew and me, inspiring restlessness, the anticipation of some great glory. And that same lifelong feeling was with me that day, the workload running in tandem with my thoughts about a new life. It was a day of energy and wellbeing, the nightmare, if I could call it that, forgotten, cowed by excitement. I considered where I might stay in London, whom I would ring, bringing the date further and further forward, reaching such a state that it was as if I was already on my way and I did not have time to tell anyone.

I skipped lunch and took money across the bar with greedy pleasure, rehearsing the role I envisaged back in the city, managing the bar in the Tremendo Club whose loud-mouthed Scottish owner I hated. He was always short of staff, but I would be tolerant and diplomatic with him. It would serve my purpose until I got fixed up somewhere else. By late afternoon I was dizzy with the prospect of my new life, annoyed that no one could appreciate my alertness, my brilliance, full of myself as I rooted around under the reception desk for the sundries order book, tossing the jumble of papers and pads around, my high reaching a point of agitation as someone pressed the buzzer impatiently above my head. I looked up through the dusty afternoon sunlight. And saw Guy.

22

Behind him a woman was struggling through the door with a pink beach bag. She looked in her early sixties, tinted glasses, white sculptured perm, acrylic cream blouse and white slacks, the breathlessness of a holidaymaker unused to Oughton's steep hills. I looked back from her to the man whose small, close eyes were fixed on me, whose jawline I had known before and who, for a further horrid moment, I thought had risen from that grave of my own making. My daylong preoccupation about my future disappeared instantly.

'We's wantin' a room. What've you got?' The accent was plain Geordie, the upward lilt of each sentence jabbing at my innards.

The woman put the bag down behind him. 'Tell him we want one with a shower.'

'A room with a shower an' two single beds.' He nodded to his side. 'Me mam, you see.'

I looked down at the desk, unable to go through the usual showy routine with the register.

'Well?' he said.

'Er . . . right. Yes, a room.' My hand was shaking. I controlled it by opening the register, running my finger down the latest handwritten entries. 'We have a room on the first floor. No sea view, I'm afraid.'

148

'An' has it a shower?'

'Yes, sir. All our rooms are en suite,' I said, my voice a remote thing, somewhere below my racing consciousness.

'And what's the charge?'

'For one night, or longer?' The words were automatic, acceptable, practised without question a thousand times before.

'Tell us the cost of both.'

'Well, it's £42.50 for one night.' He gave a soft whistle. '£75.00 for two, and pro rata. Less for the week.'

'And that includes breakfast?'

'Yes. Evening meals are extra.'

He turned to his mother. 'It's a bit steep, isn't it?'

She was looking about the lobby, craning to see into the bar. 'It's nice, though.'

The man nodded and looked back to me. 'All right. The two nights. Maybe's longer.'

'Right.'

The ritual of checking in a new arrival delivered me to a state of passable composure. I spun round the register, relaxing more by the second, now the first shock had passed. I would show them up to their room and I would be friendly. It was decent business after all – on spec customers were rare at any time of year. I pointed to the next space in the register and handed him my pen. He leaned over it. There were similarities between him and Guy, but the comparisons that had alarmed me – the slope of the shoulders, the neanderthal dome of the head, the accent – could have been made between any two men. I had not been thinking rationally. All day long, I had been a little mad. He wrote his name laboriously: *Adam* ... A fine name, biblical, reassuring. What had got into me? I should watch these mental lapses. Too many and I would

149

not be long for this world. I watched the grubby hand's slow progress across the middle column of the page. This was not Guy. . . . *Winterton.*

It was his brother.

'There's no lift then?' he said.

'No. I'm sorry.'

I led them up the stairs, stuck in the moment like a fly in amber. On the landing the floorboards creaked with a horrible familiarity. The noise spoke of transience, of the smugness of my belief that this building could be a place of protection, of my guilt. Had they been sent by Pinney? Was it coincidence, or a divinely cruel joke? The man's ambling, sniffing presence behind me was intimidating. If he was like Guy, he would have a temper. He would be an older version, steeped in crude moral codes about family loyalty. If he knew anything . . . But it might yet be nothing. In the room I was able to wait at the door, taking a good look at them while they inspected the bathroom and beds. The man, Adam, looked out of the window.

'Aye, it's fine,' he said.

His mother came up to his side, her back to me, mumbling in his ear. He nodded, took the change from his pocket and pressed two pound coins in my hand. 'There y'are. What time's breakfast?'

'Any time between seven and ten. You'll find all the details in the brochure on the table.' My voice was weak. I would have to try harder, force some politeness into my tone. 'And I might draw your attention to the fire regulations on the wall.'

'That's all right.'

I wanted to go, but my uncertainty about them later might be too poisonous to bear. And yet, couldn't I just leave them to it? Could I not trust again in the world's wheeling affairs, knowing it was up to them, if they really were Guy's family, to find me out? They might not bother me for the whole two days, keeping themselves to themselves as so many did. But I was impatient, sick to know the state of play.

'The weather,' I said, 'was quite good this morning. The forecast's for a decent day tomorrow. Are you here on holiday, sir?'

'Not as such.'

'Oh. I see.'

The mother was taking a folded raincoat and a cardigan from the top of the bag. She opened the wardrobe and took out a hanger.

'We're looking for someone,' said Adam, lighting a cigarette, watching his mother hang the coat.

I looked at his reflection in the dressing-table mirror, its dreadful reality. 'Really?'

'Aye, well. It's my brother. He's been missin' a while. We heard he'd been down here. I've got a photo somewhere. Maybe's I can show you it later.'

'Yes. Of course.' My stomach was shrinking, my head light with the starkness of the room, its apricot-flowered wallpaper, the cheap self-assembly furniture that seemed to be saying something to me, telling me I was not in the right place here, that I would soon be taken away ... 'I'd be only too pleased to help. Well, I'll leave you to it, then.' I reached for the door handle. But I could not just go. It would be too abrupt. 'There's a phone in the lobby, if you need it.' What more could I say? How could I disentangle myself from their company without making them suspicious? There were half a dozen scraps of information I might give them about the Finlandia and Oughton Bay, a catalogue of detail I could splutter out

151

until, beached by my nerves, I arrived at the one thing they had come here to find out.

'Aye, cheers,' Adam said.

It would have to do. I had to go. I closed the door and went back along the landing, the pound coins, horrendously ill-gotten, burning in my sweaty fist. One of the guests passed me, but I could only nod at his greeting. I went through the lobby and all the way outside. A fine drizzle had started. On the forecourt I tipped the plastic chairs against the tables to stop them getting wet. When I had finished, the rain had stopped and the sky was pure blue over the sea. I looked down the street at the idling, unknowing holidaymakers who were looking for something for tea, something new and tasty, fingers pointing at the baker's window, kids wheedling for burgers from a chip shop whose fatty smell was filling the air. I wanted to get among them, to share their innocence, to start walking and never come back.

23

How much could they know? They would have seen Pinney, of course. What information would he have given them? Had he the right to divulge the extent of his enquiries? Names, addresses? Some portion of the law had to be on my side, yet the family would understand its workings better than I. They were known to the police. Or might Guy's record go against them in that respect?

They went out at six. I watched from the bar as they asked Lionel if they were meant to leave their keys behind the desk, Adam's silhouette in the pale evening light, his mumbling voice giving me a fluttering sense of doom. I tried to concentrate on my duties, thinking how I might goad Lionel into taking over for the rest of the evening. But he would be away in ten minutes. It was Thursday, his night for bowls, a game Lionel cherished. The Wintertons passed the side window of the bar, heading for the Rose Gardens and the seafront. There they would find a café and, after that, a bar perhaps. It seemed too much to hope that they would not end the night back here, where they would guess, rightly, that we were easy on the hours of closing. Yet I could always hope.

Lionel came into the bar.

'It's the bowling this evening, is it, Lionel?' I asked, thinking it worth a try.

'Sure is.' He bent over, mimicking the playing of a bowl, standing and watching its imaginary progress, willing it to bend to the jack with arcing movements of his hand. 'Semifinal. You won't know it, but it's called the Alf Hawes Bowl. We're up against Brid.' He poked me in the chest. 'But we've a chance. And the telly might be doing the final. Imagine that, eh?' He took his jacket from behind the bar door.

I watched him shuffle it over his sturdy shoulders, envying him the apparently effortless simplicity of his existence. How did I manage to foul things up so much? Lionel would not have been in such a state. It would never have come to this – at some point his common sense would have intervened.

He caught me looking at him. 'You're going to be OK, are you, Harold?' The look, as ever, was sceptical, eyebrows raised, the even-toothed smile too broad, empty.

'I don't know. Perhaps you should leave your phone number in case I can't cope.' It was meant to be said in our invented joshing style, but it came out coolly.

'Don't worry, son!' He ruffled my hair, maddeningly. 'Worry never solved anything! Anyway, your mum's here. She'll look after you. Isn't that right, Peggy?'

Mother was sitting at her usual place, smiling politely at two children rolling about the floor, their parents sitting at a side table, tired and indifferent. When Mother appeared not to have heard Lionel, he left. I wished the children would be quiet, their thumps on the carpet, their yelps, had me on the point of flaring up. I went over to Mother.

'Lionel doesn't like me,' I said, the opportunity for petulance irresistible.

'And why do you think that?'

'He just doesn't. He resents me being here. It's obvious.'

The children sat down without prompting. Perhaps they had caught something of my annoyance in the air. Mother put her hand round her glass. 'He does like you, it's just that he doesn't like to show it. It's Lionel's way.'

'Is it?'

'Don't take on over him. He's been a big help to me round here. I couldn't have managed without him. And he was good with your father when he was dying.' She stared into the glass, rubbing her arm under the short sleeve of her blouse. 'He was very nice, was Lionel. Patient.'

It was another point being made against me. Where had I been when the old man was on the way out? In London, living what they thought was a life of indolence and pleasure. Christ, I felt like saying, if I'm such a shit, why does anyone even bother to speak to me? But I held my tongue, swallowing the rest of my grievances against Lionel. The outburst had been childish, though a release. I felt calmer.

'Who are the new people?' she asked.

'I don't know. They just wanted the two nights.' Talking about the Wintertons seemed to distance their threat, to share the burden. The fact that they might at that very moment be tramping around Oughton, asking about Guy, was too painful to think about. I would push it out of my mind, and if I had to speak to them, I would adopt Lionel's rough personality. The politeness I had so far shown would be revealed as a front. I did not have to care about what they were up to.

'Don't forget we're full at the weekend.'

'No.'

That was a point. *Maybe's longer.* They could only stay till Saturday morning, and that would be it. Two nights. A manageable span of time. Tomorrow I was taking Mother to an outpatient's appointment in Scarborough. With luck, we might spend most of the day away. And tomorrow night Lionel would be running the bar and I would be out with Colin.

The realisation that I only had the next few hours to worry about gave me fresh heart. My spirits lifted, my confidence shot back, a sureness in mind and limb. I would get this over with and then I would devise myself an uncluttered life, like Lionel's, devoid of enemies. I would be nice and patient with people, the idea of which imparted an almost maniacal happiness.

'You haven't forgotten about tomorrow, have you?' Mother asked.

'No. We'll go whenever you like. There's only the bakery man due. Andy can see to him.' I was relishing the prospect of the next day. It would be as good as a holiday.

The two children left the room with their mother. The father came to the bar for a pint and sat alone with it, looking out of the window at the yachts that were swaying in the bay, taking part in one of those unfathomable races where they appeared to be going nowhere. I put the money in the till.

Mother was watching as I closed the drawer with its dodgy catch. 'Do you think it's time we were computerised?'

'I can't say I've ever thought about it.'

'Reg and me had no idea about it. I could never see the point. Where are the savings in a place like this? But everyone seems to be at it. We must be the last.' She grinned. 'Even old Jack with the pet shop has one.'

'It would be expensive to start up. And why bother? If something's working all right, why try and fix it?' I didn't want to talk about this. I did not want to talk about anything.

'It was just an idea. I thought you might be quite interested in setting up something like that.'

She meant well. I hated myself for my abruptness. She was smiling, but I had hurt her, cold-bloodedly. 'I don't know. I'm no expert on that sort of thing.'

'But you must have come across them working in London.'

'Maybe I did. I probably just didn't take much notice.'

She smiled weakly. 'You're a strange lad sometimes.'

'Am I?'

'Yes, Harold. You are.' She picked up her stick and slid down from the stool.

'I'm sorry. There are one or two things on my mind at the moment. Maybe I could do with a bit of a holiday.'

'You can have that if you want, Harold. You can do as you like. You only have to say.'

I followed her slow walk along the length of the bar, imagining a little suffering to follow in the privacy of her lounge. One day, when I was in the clear, I would make it up to her. I wanted to make her happy. If there was a God, He would know I craved no more than the pleasing of the whole world, and being left to my devices.

At eight, a man Lionel had been talking to a lot recently came in and a dreary hour passed in which we only had each other's company. His name was Kelly. He was a retired car salesman who had moved to Oughton with his wife. He seemed to feel the need to get to know me, to stake out a territory at the Finlandia. My conversation was weak but it passed the time, and I was thinking of his value as a foil, should the Wintertons reappear. But he left before ten, when half a dozen of our older residents had trickled in from their evening walk on the seafront. I served and watched the clock with an impending optimism. In less than an hour, if everyone had followed their usual routine and gone up to their rooms, I would close the bar. But at ten to eleven, the Wintertons came in. The sight of them brought back all the earlier dread. They had been gone five hours, yet it seemed less than a minute.

I gave them my benign hotelier's smile. 'Good evening.'

'Yeah, evenin',' Adam slurred. He wobbled, taking a half-step back, staring drunkenly at the bar. 'I'll have, er . . .' He looked at the lager poster on the wall. 'You got any of that?'

'I'm sorry. We're out of it.'

'Oh, right. Er, what d'you want, Ma?'

Mrs Winterton nodded to the last couple in the room and seated herself in the corner. 'Just an orange. I've had enough.'

'Right. An' I'll have a whisky and Coke.'

As I made their drinks, the other customers left. I wished they hadn't. Why couldn't the bar be packed to the door? Maybe a few of the local youths would come in, chancing their arm for an after-hours drink. Tonight would be their lucky night, if they did but know it.

Adam was still standing in the middle of the room, blinking slowly, the reptilian look, with a sideways concentration, drooping head suddenly raised as if trying to stop himself falling asleep. He swerved up to the bar and dropped his change on a towel, picking out coins to pay for the drinks. He took the glasses and lurched over to his mother, leaving the rest of his money on the bar.

It was too much. I could not bear being alone with them. I slipped away to the office, taking the scotch from the desk and pouring a decent measure. I prayed they might pass through the lobby with no more than a wave and a goodnight. I switched off the tape deck, but after a minute the silence was broken by a crackling

158

strain of reggae, *Get up, stand up* ... I hung around by the doorway to the bar, pretending to check the bottle stock list. Adam had produced a small black radio and put it on the table. Mrs Winterton was sniffling into a handkerchief, her son trying to calm her, his arm round her shoulders in the oversolicitous manner of the drunk. He was trying to get her to have another drink, saying it would make her feel better. She shook her head, put her bag over her shoulder and left the room. Adam remained, sitting on the wall seat, legs sprawled, briefly attempting to follow the beat of the music with his head. Then he turned off the radio and came awkwardly up to the bar where he had left his money. He scowled at the coins. 'Same again, mate, please.'

I made his drink, catching the optic a second time in the hope that this would be enough for him. 'Is your mother all right?'

He lifted his hand and let it drop, as if the question was too much trouble. 'She's upset. Who wouldn't be? She's lost her son. My brother. Vanished off the face of the earth,' he said with a boozy gravity.

My cheeks flushed. I busied myself until it passed.

'It's a right fucking shitty game,' he said angrily, making my heart stir.

'Yes, it sounds dreadful,' I said, selecting my words carefully. 'Haven't you told the police?'

He grimaced. 'Hah, fat lot of use, those bastards!' He was concentrating hard on pulling something from his inside jacket pocket. 'Here. This is him. His name's Guy. He's a good lad. And he's bloody missing.'

The mention of Guy's name raised the stakes. I set my teeth as he handed me a photograph. It showed Guy in the countryside, perhaps the Lakes. He was wearing hiking gear, rucksack, checked shirt, walking boots. He looked much younger, no more than fifteen. I tilted it to the light, making a show of studying it closely, and handed it back. 'I'm sorry, I don't recognise him.'

'That's what everybody says. This bloody town! He was here.' His eyes were closed and he was rocking with the pulse of his blood. 'He was bloody here, and nobody'll say they saw him. No one gives a shit.'

I was standing two feet from him, my relative sobriety giving me a handy feeling of condescension. I was trying to think how I might get him to go. But he pulled Mother's stool from the end of the bar and sat down, leaning on his elbow, pointing at me. 'What's your name?'

'Harold.'

'Harold what?'

I smiled wearily. 'People just call me Harold.'

'You've got another name. What is it?'

Would Pinney have given him Maisie's name? It was my first moment of panic, but with luck, and his drunkenness, I might get away with a small lie. 'Baker.'

Adam studied his glass with a leery smile, the conformation of his teeth the same as his brother's, appallingly familiar. I wished he would take a drink, just to change that expression. 'Harold Baker. Knows nothing.' He snorted. 'Harold Baker. Innocent man. Ignor-ant.' He took a sip and winced. 'You're sad, you are, Harold.'

'Am I?'

''S right. You're fucking sad, man. Sad.'

'If you say so,' I said, trying to humour him, as I had a thousand drunks in my time.

'I do. It's right. You're . . .' He was smiling, waving his finger at me. 'You say it. Go on. What are you, Harold? What sort of man are you?'

160

'Oh, come on – '

'Say it!'

He was staring, but he would be no match for the anger I felt. The moment was heavy with silence. I was breathing heavily.

'Go on,' he said. 'What are you, Harold Baker?'

I smiled with a grudging effeteness, giving him all the ground he wanted. 'I'm a sad man. All right?'

He tipped the glass against his lips, laughing to himself. 'Ah, you're all right, you are, Harold. You're all right.'

I couldn't stand it any longer. I moved away and turned off the wall lights in the room. 'Will you be having another drink, sir?' I said, as coldly as I could.

He looked up from his animal ruminations, as if unsure who was speaking to him. 'What?'

'Another drink? I shall have to close the bar shortly.'

It was the right approach. He was used to the vagaries of English closing time, being shown the door by the landlord. He emptied the glass, screwed up his eyes and shook his head. 'Christ, that's . . . I think that's my lot. For today, anyways.' He picked up the coins one by one, dropping them in his pocket. 'But tomorrow, Harold, old mate, I'm goin' to find him. No one'll stop me.' He went back to the table and picked up his radio. On his swerving way to the door he stopped. 'Where there's a will, Harold . . .' He was waving the radio in an insistent gesture, wobbling on his feet. 'Where there's a will, there's a bloody way. Am I right?'

'If you say so,' I said. 'Goodnight.'

'Yeah, right,' he said grinning, trying to get the radio into his pocket. 'Right, old mate. Right.'

I listened as he went past the reception desk and made his way up the stairs, one clumping step at a time.

161

24

They were down for breakfast at seven thirty, the sight of them turning my stomach. I had hoped to avoid them, to have got Mother ready and away before they surfaced. But there was Adam hunched over a plate of eggs, bacon and sausages, the constitution of a labourer. And yes, it could have been Guy the night I saw him in the Burnt Offerings, devouring his chilli, sustenance for the dissolute, getting his money's worth. Mrs Winterton was eating more daintily, self-consciously, a wary eye on Mary who was straightening cutlery on the rest of the tables. I passed quickly through the room. Today I would have to let Mary get on with the serving herself. I would make some excuse about getting the car out to attend to the oil. She came into the kitchen and I was about to explain this to her when Adam shouted from the dining room.

'Harold!'

Mary looked at me.

'Mr Baker!'

I raised my eyes to the heavens. 'He's a pain,' I muttered. 'This man is an absolute nuisance.'

'Why did he call you that?'

'I don't know.'

'I went into the dining room, bending over their table,

obscuring Adam from Mary's view. 'Good morning. Did you sleep well?'

'Sound, Harold. Sound.' He was chewing as he spoke. 'Hey, we were just saying, we know a family called Baker in Scarborough. No relation, are you, Harold?'

'I wouldn't think so. It's a very common name.'

'There,' said Mrs Winterton. 'Told you.'

'No 'arm in asking, is there?'

I straightened up to move away. 'Well, if you'll excuse me – '

'Wait.' Adam reached into his jeans pocket and pulled out a crumpled piece of yellow notepaper. 'We're wantin' this address. D'you know it?'

He smoothed out the paper and handed it to me. It had Maisie's name on it, and the address of Matthew's house. Pinney must have given it to them, perhaps to get them off his back. Or was it a deliberate move? The rich poison of paranoia stirred in me, not for the first time. This was a tedious, elaborate charade. They were so close to the truth it was laughable. These two knew exactly who I was. Their relationship with Pinney was perfectly wholesome. He had sent them to work on me. I looked round. Mary was coming this way. I folded the paper and handed it back, knowing I could not lie. They would only have to ask Mary, or go into the first shop they saw, to get the right directions. On foot, they would be there in fifteen minutes. Mary passed by to set the table in the corner.

'If you turn right out of here, go along to the top road, go left for about half a mile, you'll see it on the right.'

'Cheers, Harold.' He stuffed the paper back in his pocket. 'You're a star.'

On my way out of the room I spoke with Mary. 'They're

163

trouble. Take no nonsense from them. The sooner they're out of here, the better. Right?'

Mary looked across at them, but gave no sign of agreeing with me. The damn woman, why couldn't she be on my side? Why couldn't she at least smile, just this once?

I went through the kitchen, ignoring Andy's bemused glance, and out to the garage to feign working on the car, to let my heart slow down.

Mother came down at half past eight, fussing over the cardigan and slacks she had chosen to wear. The Wintertons were back upstairs, preparing to go out. Within an hour they would be at Matthew's house, making blunt enquiries of the neighbours, if they were there, or the Charltons. This chatterbox pair were my biggest worry. They would tell them about the family connection, the Finlandia the Wintertons had so stupidly wandered into. Why couldn't they have stayed at the Ship? Or at one of the pubs for half the price? They would have been so much happier there!

They had gone out by the time Mother was ready. We got in the car and I drove to the top road, looking along the direction in which they should have been heading. But there was no sign of them. Perhaps they were there already, Adam looking stern, the right fist clenched with my face in mind. The idea imparted a grim humour. The man was so obtuse. And I pictured a risible scene with the pair of us tumbling about the hotel lobby. Or maybe I was worrying over nothing? Worry never solved anything. I drove on in silence.

At Scarborough I went into the hospital and up to the second floor to wait with Mother. When her name was called, she rose from her seat in a mood of happy anticipation, like a child on Christmas morning. It both irritated me and helped defuse my own black ponderings.

Indeed, the hospital itself was having a curiously relaxing effect on me. From the window I could see an ambulance bringing a desperate-looking stretcher case, the body so swaddled in orange blankets and an oxygen mask that you could not tell its age or sex. Inside, the porters and nurses were passing by with varying degrees of urgency. These people were so important. Why had I never thought of such work as this? And the air smelled of linen, an overlay of polish. Such a beautiful, necessary place. I could never understand why people found hospitals gloomy.

These were dreamy moments, my earlier tension turning crusty, only effortfully remembered. Though the truth may have been that people could already be looking for me. Perhaps the Wintertons, with gross good fortune, had come across Colin on his rounds? Colin in a menopausal and disloyal mood, squinting at the photograph, remembering that night in the Trawlerman's, remembering that day at the age of ten and the one who had really booted the ball over the wall and smashed the cold frame. I pictured all this happening, urgent phone calls, a nettled Pinney leaping into his car for a screaming drive south, an irate Adam pacing the hotel lobby, an assortment of local policemen bemused by his allegations of the weird happenings on their patch. I saw myself being led to a car, perhaps asked to pose for a photograph for the local rag. Should I smile impassively, or should I look sinister, the grizzly digger of the east coast? I stared at a porter passing with an empty trolley, then looked down at my shoes on the shiny floor. Whose laws had I broken anyway? I didn't invent them. I had been born a free organic unit, part of the evolutionary process. The legal system was devised by other men's minds. Why accept their version of right and wrong? It was the fag end of my concerns. The optimism had run out. I was tired of it. Now it was simply down to luck, the fall of the cards directing the path I must follow, without a murmur of dissent.

An hour later, back in the car, Mother was jamming on the seat belt. 'Mr Flett says it's the last time. He says he doesn't need to see me any more.'

My mind was empty now, with thoughts only for starting the engine and concentrating on the manoeuvre out of the packed car park. 'Isn't that good?'

'No, I don't think it is. I told him about the soreness I get at night. It has me in tears, I told him so. He just didn't want to know. It could be that osteoporosis, I said. Maybe he should test for it. But he wouldn't hear of it. That's the trouble with young doctors, they've no idea what being old is like. They don't know what you go through. It's all theory with them. They haven't lived long enough to understand.'

She took a tissue from her bag. I knew her small depressions, the greyness that would descend for days, the long lie-ins, the refusal to eat properly, the sulks. At seventy years of age. Do we never grow up?

'Maybe we could get you to see someone else,' I said. 'Isn't there somewhere private you could go?'

'Hah! And who would I see? Probably Flett again, doing a moonlight. They're all on that game. I don't think you get any truly private doctors. At least, nobody you can trust. You're stuck with the Health Service. And what does that amount to, these days?'

'Couldn't we ask around?'

'No. If it appears I'm not worth the bother, then so be it. Take me home, Harold. I've had enough for one day.'

For some reason, I felt in a consoling mood. The act of talking was a remote easy task. 'Maybe you just need

166

something to take your mind off it? Why don't you take up your painting again?'

She said nothing, looking hurt, as if she had been waiting for this encouragement for years. I had compounded her disaffection. It did not seem a decent moment to suggest a tour of the shops to delay the return home.

It was only twenty past eleven. We would be back in Oughton before twelve. But the bizarre upward shift in my mood had found a new level. The excursion, my dangerous musings of half an hour before, had woken me up. Now I felt recovered, prepared for anything. And so far, what had actually gone wrong? I had given Adam a false name. And what could such a cretin hope to achieve on his own? He was not the police, who, quite probably, had given up looking for Guy anyway. This could genuinely be my last problem. True, it might be uncomfortable if Adam had discovered my relationship with Maisie, but couldn't I get my act together one last time? It would be easy enough to say my niece had suffered badly at the hands of the police, that she couldn't help them and I had only wanted to protect her from any more needless enquiries. Surely, I would say in a firm middle-class tone, he could understand that? I should think of these things, I told myself. Be positive. The game was a long way from being up. Watch the time, mark its passing. It might yet be the only hurdle left.

Mother remained quiet. I drove out of the north side of town, thinking to take a more circuitous route back to Oughton, remarking on the roadworks on the way here that had made Mother fret she might be late. She did not object.

I drove across the main coast road to the countryside and narrow lanes beyond. The villages were quiet. Dying, I thought, in this mortally wounded piece of England. A

167

sliver of the previous day's ambition returned. I would have to get away from here. It was making me old before my time. The idea was uplifting, once again giving me a future to consider. I was only thirty-nine. Still young. Years of youth to look forward to. It was a matter of choice.

At a crossroads I realised that if I turned left I would be back in Scarborough, and going right would mean a journey of at least ten miles before I could find a way back towards Oughton. I could only carry on ahead, the road taking me past the wood where I had buried Guy. I had not been near since that day. It was something I could never have faced. Yet now it was unavoidable. I would try not to think about it.

We descended the dip into Carnham, following the road with its thick hawthorn borders, through Hastow and over the green hill towards the wood. Ahead was the bend that would take us past the five-barred gate. The road was narrow and unmarked. I had no option but to slow down. And I almost stopped when I saw that the gate and a section of the fence had been removed.

Along the track between the trees was a line of vehicles, the furthermost of which was a yellow digger, clanking and wheezing, its shovel nose worrying at the ground.

PART THREE

25

I reversed back to the entrance to the wood. 'What are they doing?'

'Heavens, Harold! I don't know. They'll be cutting down the trees. Does it matter?'

Along the track were two closed wagons, a double-section open lorry and a metallic blue Metro estate. Apart from the man working the digger, I could see two others, one watching the digger's progress and pointing at the ground, the other carrying a pile of staves, laying them individually on the grass at roughly regular intervals. Their yellow helmets gave them an air of officialdom. Of nemesis.

Mother sighed. I wanted to blame her for everything. She had brought me into this world. She had brought me to this day. Without her, I would not have had the encumbrance of family loyalty. I would not have done what I had done. 'But why?' I said, my voice rising. 'Why are they cutting them down?'

'Dear God, that's what they do. For the timber. It's what all these woods round here are for. I thought you'd know that.'

'But I thought it was National Trust.' I was protesting helplessly.

'It is. But the arrangement is that they plant two trees

for every one they take up. Seems a reasonable gesture to nature to me.'

From what I could see, the far quarter of the wood was ravaged as a battlefield, the digger dragging up the stumps of the trees that had already been cut. The clods of dried mud on the road suggested they had been there for days, working systematically back along the left-hand side. Guy was on the right.

My scalp ran cold, the malaise of apprehension returning like a symptom of some chronic illness.

'Harold, are we staying here all day? I don't feel so good.'

'No. We're going.'

I started up the car, wanting to get away, to think this through. It was just another foul coincidence, the world conspiring against me one more time. Yet I was the only one who knew Guy was there. It was my secret, a big ballooning thing inside me, taking over my brain.

Or had he been found? By a man walking his dog? Or one of those nerdy people with metal detectors who swept their stooped unspeaking way over sands and fields? But that was impossible. Where were the police? And what would have been the point in hacking the wood to bits? I saw a name along the side of one of the wagons: J. F. Clayton, Landscape Contractor. I had to believe that their presence here was innocent. My discovery of them was a stroke of fate.

Mother looked down at her hands, ahead at the road. 'You know, Harold, sometimes I just can't keep up with you. You get in the strangest moods.'

'Do I?'

'Yes. It's as if you've always got something on your mind, a problem you can't bear to trust anyone with. I

172

know what it is. You're at that funny age for a man. You wouldn't know it, but for a while Reg went completely off the rails – '

'Mother, I don't want to hear about it. All right?'

'I was only saying, your father was just the same – '

'Mother, will you be quiet! It's not my bloody age. It's not anything. Just leave it!'

She looked in front of her, pale, her breath taken. I was in no mood for apology. I rammed the car into gear, took one last glimpse at the wood, and drove away in furious silence.

The next few hours passed in confusion, the time beyond my grasp. In a daze, a ghost of myself, I decided to prepare the rooms for the next day's arrivals, hoping at least to stay out of the Wintertons' way. They were a problem that would have to look after itself, an imminent threat to which I could give no more consideration, the worry so great that I had to avoid it. I brought towels and sheets from the linen cupboard and put soap and shampoos in the shower rooms. I hoovered, I opened the windows to each of the seven rooms I was attending, careful not to be found lingering near the one taken by the Wintertons. (If only they would go, just leave me alone . . .) The activity would pass the time, keep me insulated from everyone until I could think straight. I did not want to speak to a soul. I was not capable of conversation. The men in the woods dominated my mind, their meddlesome work, the atrocious find that was coming their way if I did not muster the energy to intervene. But the immediacy of the situation was too much to bear. I was not prepared for it. I polished handbasins obsessively, dusting dressers and windowsills that did not need doing. The work was not helping, but I could not stop. I thought of the hundreds of bodies that had passed through these rooms, sleeping, screwing, crapping here. They would not come again, not when the headlines hit the newspapers, or the television crews had taken their pictures. What would become of me, of us all?

It was midafternoon. The prospect of Guy being found was more real than it had ever been. Before it had simply been a matter of parrying the odd enquiry, like Pinney's or even the Wintertons'. Now I felt shamed by the optimism that had kept me going for so long. It had been a vanity, a conceit. And now it could only be a matter of time, a few days at most, before it was all over. In room 9 I checked drawers, slamming them shut. I picked up the pillows and threw them at the wall. It was satisfying. I looked around for anything I could smash, picking up a bedside lamp, feeling its fake onyx stem in my crushing fist . . .

This was pointless. If I could have wept, I would have. But I was not the crying kind. My emotions were rarely so accessible. A lifetime of English male suppression had seen to that. True, there were times when I was so excited I was almost out of control. And there were days of a stuporous indifference to life. But this, melodrama, was not my way. Besides, I would have had to unplug the lamp before it went anywhere. Foolish man! I put the lamp down and sat on the bed, lonely and sorry for myself.

If I could not face going back to the wood, there were two more options. Either I could run away, making a start that very hour, or I would wait here until they came for me. The first had a certain romantic appeal. A few weeks on the run would make for a very intense existence, a screaming-pitch appreciation of the essence of survival, being alive. But what talents, what energy did I have for

174

such an escapade? I would be found as all fugitives were, crazed and starving, holed up in some awful derelict house. It would be a farce. And where would I run to anyway? The second choice was more likely, more like me, the bungler, a bit of a coward. Yet I truly did not want to be caught. Or, more precisely, in that instant of self-pity, I did not want to be shown up for the ass I had become. And with this wish I dispensed with both ideas. There was no getting away from it, no other answer. I would have to move Guy. I forced myself to realise that still nothing had happened. I was not to blame for the way things had gone. It had been bad luck, lousy luck. You make your own luck in this life. A dreary saying of my father's. But I did have one last chance to make amends, to fight for my freedom.

I looked up and saw Lionel standing in the doorway.

He looked at the pillows on the floor, the lamp on its side. A wild breeze was blowing through the window, making the curtains fly. He smiled, seeing my madness, something he had an eye for. 'Sorry, Harold, mate. There's a call for you.'

'Who is it?'

'I think it's your niece.'

I looked around the room, hopelessly trying to give the impression that the mess had some purpose. 'Right. I'll take it in Mother's room. Thank you, Lionel.'

He hung around in the doorway for a few seconds, the smile fading to something like concern. 'Are you all right, Harold?'

'Yes, I'm fine.'

He nodded, tapped the doorframe playfully with his knuckle, and went back along the landing. I went up the stairs, checked Mother's bedroom to make sure she was not there, and went into her lounge. I sat on the sofa and picked up the phone.

'Maisie?' The line clicked as Lionel put down the receiver on the office phone.

'Oh, Harold, I'm sorry to ring you.' Her voice broke. Until that moment I had not thought what the call might be about. It could not be important, there was no more weight that could be brought on my shoulders, nothing else I could carry. 'I just had to call you.'

'What's the matter?'

'I just feel so bad.'

'What do you mean?' I was being sharp. It couldn't be helped. The aborted rage of a few minutes before came back, a different strain, ripened and wilful. Speaking to someone gave me a new target.

'I don't know. I keep having these nightmares about Guy coming back. Then I wake up and I think they're going to find him and take me away . . . I can't help it.' She was sobbing.

The mention of Guy's name stilled the anger. I would have to be calm, to give nothing away. 'That's silly, Maisie. A few weeks ago you were fine.'

'I know. It was all right when you were here. You helped. But I can't rely on you for ever.'

'Why not? I'm here, aren't I?'

'No. I know I have to go it alone. But I can't. It's just too hard for me on my own. I keep wanting to tell someone about it. It never seems to get any better, just going on and on, this horrible feeling. Harold?'

'What?'

She sighed. 'I think we should go to the police.'

'No!'

'It's the only way I'll ever feel right again. I can't live with myself – '

'You can, Maisie. You must. What would be the point in giving up now? We're virtually in the clear.' I wanted to laugh at my own lie. The mess I was in! The almost supernatural forces that were unifying against me, bringing the matter to a head. But a crazy wisdom was on me, the need for seeing the funny side of it all. I held it back.

'I'm so upset . . .'

'It'll be like that,' I said. 'But only for a while.'

'I don't think so. It'll never end.'

I held the receiver a few inches away, trying to think, tired of Maisie's raw conscience. In her place, Nicola would not have felt guilt. She would have been over the whole incident in an hour, brilliantly so, negating all personal responsibility, with a little shopping later to reaffirm her view of the world and all she thought it owed her. I was about to produce another platitude when I heard the rattling rivets of Mother's stick outside the door. She put her head round. 'Sorry, Harold. Will you be long?'

'Another few minutes.' I spoke so that Maisie would know there was someone here. I was tired of placating her, wanting some conjuror's trick to make her see sense and go away.

'Who's that?'

'Just your gran.'

'Harold – '

'Listen, Maisie. Why don't you come up here for the weekend? We could talk.' It was a delaying tactic. I hoped she would not come. Tomorrow I might be busy . . .

'I've told you what I want to do.'

'I know what you want. But have you thought about my part in all this? I've a lot to lose too, you know. Maybe more

177

than you realise.' It was the first time I had used this line. It was mean, an admission of weakness. She seemed about to say something, then stopped. 'Look, Maisie, what I'm saying is, don't do anything on your own. These things have to be thought through. Running to the police would only be a temporary solution to the way you feel, but it might have some very permanent effects. Try and think about that.' My articulacy surprised me. For a brief second, in all the craziness of the day, I felt I was more intelligent than I gave myself credit for.

'I feel so useless. I don't want to get you into trouble. It wouldn't matter what you did. You'd be in the clear.'

A long debate was called for, but I did not have the will for it. 'I don't think it would be that simple. Maisie, I don't want to seem hard, but I want you to get a grip. Give it just two more days. I'll come and see you again.'

'I don't want that – '

'Well, come up here, then. We have to talk.'

She sighed again. It was an irritating sound, the petulance of a spoilt child. 'All right, all right. I'm sorry. I promise I won't do anything. I just had to speak to you. I get to the end of my tether.'

Had the impulse passed? It seemed too easy, yet the friability of her moods was something I was learning about Maisie. Maybe there was some truth in what Mother had told me about her. 'Yes. I understand that. But do try and remember yours is only half the part in all this. Look, I'm always here. Maisie, I'm on your side.' I was working hard to conceal my relief. She gave an odd groan. 'Bide your time, Maisie. Please?'

'I . . . All right. A bit longer. We'll have to meet, though. And soon.'

178

'We will. Don't worry about that. Now, do you want to talk some more? Or shall I ring you back later?'

'No, no. I'm OK now.'

'You're sure?'

'Yes.'

'Look, I'll ring you tomorrow night.'

'Yes. All right.'

She put down the phone.

Mother came into the room. I stood. 'Finished now,' I said, with an improbable cheerfulness.

She limped to the side of her chair, keeping a wary distance between us. 'And how is Maisie?'

'She's OK. She's fine.'

Mother looked away, still stinging from my outburst that morning. It was a breach in our mutual trust that might take a long time to mend. For now, I did not have the time to build bridges. I went to the bathroom to rinse my face.

I had not handled Maisie at all well. I saw her feelings lurching again, the half-child with no capacity yet for carrying the hardships of life. There would be a dash along the streets to the police, perhaps no more than a phone call, the least effortful way to rid her of her burden. As if life would then be rosy and pure again – a dialled number and all her pains instantly relieved. But I could not have dealt with her any other way. It was not my fault. She had picked the wrong time. It would be good to explain this to her one day, but I would never be able to.

I went down the stairs thinking my problems had a life of their own. Getting too stressed by them would finish me off. And yet there was no release. I wanted to snatch up the last six months of my life like a piece of paper, rip it up and start again. But I couldn't. I was trapped in it. And my head was aching, a piece of metal clamped along one side of my skull as I entered the lobby and saw Adam standing at the desk. Beside him was his mother, the stuffed pink bag at her feet.

26

There was no avoiding them. Adam trapped me with his glare. I had little appetite for continuing my charade with him, yet what else could I do? For a few desperate seconds I would still have to hope they had discovered nothing. I stayed at the foot of the stairs. 'Are you going out for the day?'

Adam hissed through his teeth. I was an object of loathing, pond life. 'Told us a right tale, didn't you?'

'I'm sorry?'

'Mr Baker?'

I held his look, buoyed by an annoyance with him that shielded me from his anger. I was every inch a manifestation of middle-class duplicity, but it suited me.

'You's know that girl, don't you?' he said. 'She's your niece, I'm told.'

Lionel was leaning with his palms flat on the desk, sleeves rolled up. The muscles in his forearms emboldened me. They were an asset of the establishment, paid for on a weekly basis. He was an ex-soldier, a Falklands veteran. For him, dealing with this youth would be simplicity itself. And his duty. But he stood back, folding his arms over his belly, looking at me for a response as if he had taken Adam's side. I said, 'I had my reasons.' But my prepared argument about wanting to protect Maisie seemed weak. Adam shifted his weight from one trainered foot to the other, taking an offensive stance that made Lionel smile.

'He wants his money back,' Lionel said. 'I've explained it's not hotel policy to give refunds for nights already paid for.'

'Pay him.'

'But we don't do that, Harold.'

'Give them their money back.'

'An' I want it all,' Adam said.

Lionel huffed and looked to the ceiling.

'Give him it,' I said.

Lionel shook his head and pinged open the till. Adam pointed at me. 'You're a bastard, d'you know that? Your sort . . . ah, you're shit, man.' His mother shifted uneasily, touching her glasses, clasping her arms around her.

At that moment I could have turned away, but the confrontation had taken a hold. I recklessly fancied my chances. My face flushed with the challenge. I wanted to reinforce the social standing he so plainly hated, to wind him up. 'Please don't use that language here.'

'I'll say what I like. An' listen, I've tumbled you, see? You know somethin' about our Guy.' He took a step towards me, a gesture that softened my flickering bravery. Then Lionel tapped his arm, holding out the money.

'Here,' Lionel said. 'You've got what you want.'

Adam took the notes, jammed them in his pocket and snatched up the bag. He was past the sharpest point of his hostility. And outnumbered. 'You've not heard the last of me. Got that? I'm gonna get to the bottom of this. And fast. I'm gonna find out what happened to my brother. You're swinging for this, sunshine. Dead meat, you.' From the department of empty threats. Face-saving blather. I turned away, heading for the kitchen. Adam called behind my back, 'There's gonna be people lookin' for you, Broome. Or is it Baker, eh?'

In the kitchen I drew a deep breath. The room was empty, the only sound coming from the extractor fan on the side wall. I pulled the cord to turn it off and leaned on the worktop, taking even, regular breaths. The aggression had drained me. Then, through the dusty side window, I saw them leave, Guy's relatives, making their scuttling argumentative departure along the drive of the Finlandia and into the street.

Colin laughed, pleased with himself. 'Too immature. That's what she said. I couldn't believe it. God, kids!'

'Who said?'

'Sally. My girl. Christ, Harold, are you listening or what?'

He chuckled again. The bar of the Rose was full with a party of sea anglers, eight or nine men with gruelly South Yorkshire accents, beer-gutted and denimed, here for a weekend away from their wives. Both the television and the jukebox were booming at their request, and from the fruit machine came the repeated opening bars of *EastEnders*. For once, Colin did not seem to notice the row.

'It was last night. She came storming into the house, dropped on the settee and said – get this – "That's it. I've ditched him. He's too childish for me. If all lads are like that, I don't want to know." And her only thirteen! Music to my ears, Harold, I can tell you.'

I could not bear to look at his satisfied smile. His happiness was vulgar, shoddy like his brown slip-on shoes and his off-the-peg suit. I hated Colin. I was glad that I had got him into trouble at school. After tonight, I never wanted

183

to see him again. In fact, I wanted to leave Oughton by the end of next week, if not before.

'And what've you been up to this week?' he asked.

'Nothing to report.'

He turned to me, looking closely with his quasi-medical concern. 'You look a bit peaky, old mate. You want to look after yourself a bit more.'

'Do I?'

The anglers were leaving, scraping chairs and joshing loudly, the sea air livening their aspirations. The last of them downed a full pint, belched, wiped his mouth and chased past the window after his mates. They left their smoke on the air. Despite all my distaste for them, I wished they had not gone. Now there was only me and Colin, and the domino school whose usual squabbling had been cowed by the visitors.

'Why don't you come to the golf club some time?' Colin asked.

'It's not my thing, really.'

'Ah, bull! You'd like it. What're you up to tomorrow?'

'Working.'

'What about first thing?'

'It's my lie-in on Saturdays.'

'Lie-in, balls! You want to get out, get a bit of colour in your cheeks.'

'Colin, I can't stand golf.'

'You'd like it if you tried. You've spent too much time in the city, old son.'

It was his way of getting at me. No wonder his only real friends were old ladies. I wanted to tell him to shut up; it was my direst need. After a while, he seemed to get the message. He went to the bar, asking for the noise to be turned down, laughing with the girl, forcing his good

184

mood on her. For me, at least it was respite from the effort of conversation. I should have stayed at home, but that might have been worse with Lionel there, triumphant over the way Adam had shown me up, glowing with the intrigue of a missing youth. And there would be Mother, nursing her sulky depression, puzzling over my anger towards her, seeking the solace of anyone who might listen. My gaze dropped to my shoes, a favourite pair of expensive brogues I had bought at a country outfitters in Chelsea. It was comforting to look at them, to be reminded of a better life than this. Nicola apart, why had I left London? Bloody panic. Sentiment. Here, I was losing my identity. I deserved better than Oughton and its small-minded people whose chief pleasure was to bait anyone who wished for a better life.

Colin was coming back from the bar. It was nine thirty. I was torn between making this drink the last, and having a skinful. Yet I did not think I could get drunk. And tomorrow was the day, I knew grimly, when I would have to make good my central folly, a last act before I quit this place. On Saturdays workmen, builders, tree-cutters alike took a day of rest. And I was going to move Guy, or whatever remained of him, and bury him out on the moors, so deep that he could never be found. And that would be that. It was all I had energy left for. The rest would be a matter for the gods and how they chose to treat me.

'I said to that girl behind the bar that it was quiet now. She said she hoped it would go on that way, then she'd have less to do. The attitude of them, eh?' Colin was standing in front of me, the tip of his tie and his soft belly inches from my face. I could smell the boiled-potato sweat of his working life. 'Cheer up, Harold! God, have you forgotten how to smile, or what?'

27

'You've ruined my life.'

'Nicola, you can't say that. It's not true.'

'You have. It's what you wanted to do to me.'

It is the first time I have seen her for two weeks. Am I still hoping something might come of this? That there may be one more chance? She is wearing that pretty, dusty pink jacket. It does not suit her mood. Has she come back with other intentions, reconciliation perhaps? For days I have been fielding the bills, the threat of court orders. The woman at the Citizens Advice Bureau has said, Be a bankrupt. And the house we were making together has died. It's the home of a male now, logically ordered, sterile, as my flat used to be. Nicola stuffs a few things into carrier bags, then stops. She comes up behind where I am sitting and thumps me on the head. She slaps.

She screeches, 'I'll fucking kill you! You bastard, I hate you. Hate you!'

I grab hold of her wrists. There's that same mad dying in her eyes, the same look that once said, I want it to hurt.

'Nicola, you're doing this to yourself. You don't know what you want.' I say, slowly, 'It is not my fault.'

Her eyes are closed, the face bunched against this truth. There may yet be a chance, we both know it. She tugs herself away from me, hardens her jaw in spite. 'I'm going. I never want to see you again. I couldn't bear to look at you again.'

She snatches up a few things and goes, the front door slamming tediously.

Through the net-curtained lounge window I see a man and a woman leaving the house opposite. She has a pageboy blonde hairstyle, decades out of date, like her white imitation-fur coat, the black high heels. A rough piece, but contented. The man puts his arm around her and kisses her cheek as they walk away. I do not know them. There is no one round here I could ever get to know. I have been here too long and failed too often, in love, work, trying to be happy. Time to admit defeat, to try again. But where?

And for the first time in eighteen years I realise I am a long way from home.

It was seven o'clock. I walked along the landing, hearing the guests stirring, a television on, a fart, a man singing as he washed. The smells of breakfast had filtered up from downstairs and my tread was easy, light on the carpet. I had slept better than expected, a good six hours. In the kitchen I found Andy bright and busy in his white apron.

'Looks like a damp one, Harold,' he said, glancing up at the sky through the window. 'Coffee?'

'Yes. Thank you.'

'You're up early.'

'I know, well, one or two things to do.'

He had lined up sausages and strips of bacon on his chopping board, and now he was slicing off the rind in single strokes, following the contours of the meat with artistic precision, laying the slices in the sizzling pan. 'Where was it last night, then?'

'The Rose.'

'I thought the Trawlerman's was your place of a Friday?'

'It used to be. We've switched.'

I felt soft and lazy. I could have hung around like this all morning, watching Andy about his work, his sense of purpose and economy, catching what I might of a younger man's aspirations, the things that pleased him. It was a dream state, a holding, protective indifference to the fact that I was about to perform the most revolting act of my life. I chatted with him for a few more minutes, then stirred myself and went outside before Mother came down.

It was a grey morning, warm and close, and I put the spade and pick and one of the hotel's white sheets in the car. My movements were mechanical, without thought. It felt like a routine matter, as if I was going to work on someone's garden for the morning. I had not bothered to make any excuses about where I was going. It did not seem necessary. In our brief talk, Andy and I had got on better than I could remember. In a bizarre way, it was almost as if our chef knew what I had to do and was tacitly sympathetic. This was surreal thinking. It got me through the first stage of the morning, and maybe it would help me through the awfulness of what was to come. I would recover my sanity later. I got into the car and drove away from the Finlandia, out of Oughton.

The weekend traffic was thin, the trippers no doubt deterred by the scudding clouds, the mucky northerly wind that rippled the fields of wheat and rape away over the Wolds. It was only fifteen minutes later, as I saw the turn-off ahead, that I felt a thump of naked reality, the air thick in my chest. But even that passed. I was wise to all this, experienced. I, my alter ego, had done it before. I turned off the main road and along to the wood.

Of the line of vehicles I had seen, only two remained. The digger was parked at the near end of the cleared area, lifted up on its shovel, front wheels in the air. Alongside it was the dumper, at an angle, as if it had been abandoned the moment the shift was over. The lorries were gone, but they had left deep ruts in the track that made it difficult to get as close as I wanted. I bounced the car along the track and into the grass on the right-hand side, a few yards short of where I thought I had parked the last time. A small panic came over me as I wondered if I had got the car stuck. I would not be able to move it alone. Was I as in control as I believed? But when I got out, I saw that my fear was unfounded. The tracks I had made in the grass were flat, easy to negotiate in reverse. I looked around, remembering the man with the shotgun, thinking he would not be around, thanks to the attentions of the workmen. I took a deep breath and even smiled to myself as I took the spade and the folded sheet from the boot. I put on my boots and gloves, picked up my things, had one last look around to make sure I was alone, and set off into the wood.

The grass was tall and thick with a few peeping bluebells and a whiff of garlic. Further in, the undergrowth became suddenly sparse. At first I thought I could not find the exact spot, my memory suspect, holding only stark and unreliable images of pine trees, brambles, a hollow in the floor of the wood. The details of my dreams. A little mental dissembling threatened, an overalertness. Then I found the fallen tree, the area more enclosed than I could recall, which I put down to the summer growth of vegetation. The brambles were thriving everywhere and the wind in the treetops rushed

189

like the sea. Had my earlier work been good enough? Did I really need to go through with this? The old lassitude came back. I could keep my hands clean and take a chance. They might not find it. Then I saw the mud on the log where I had scraped clay off the spade. The rain had not done its job. The fact of the smears stung me, waking me up to the task at hand. There was no avoiding this. I pushed the brambles with the spade and they rolled neatly back. My face tingled with the realisation that my efforts had been much less competent than I had believed. I could see the outline of the grave where the covering earth had sunk a few inches. Orange clay was speckled about the loamy surface. Had the lime done its job? I flexed my arms and opened my mouth to take a few deep breaths. Looking back through the trees and the filigree of branches and tall grass at the wood's edge, I could see only a few shards of yellow; the digger, seventy yards away. I took up the spade.

The top few inches lifted easily, the soil having melted together only lightly with the effects of dew and rain. I decided to pace myself, remembering the frantic effort this had taken the first time round. I probed at a central section, thinking my memory might not be reliable over the position I had left Guy in. The first revelation of whatever was left might show me where to dig next. Then the spade stopped on something lumpy, the area I guessed would be the ribcage. I paused, dizzy. It took a minute to clear. I told myself I must not be sick. I had to stay on top of things, to be manly. It was only a matter of time. If I concentrated on the passing seconds, on the twenty minutes I thought the job would take me, I would be all right. I would survive.

I straddled the impression in the ground and the foot-deep hole I had shovelled out. I prepared myself for the first sign of decayed flesh, bones and coloured organs. From the

190

freshly turned soil I thought I caught a whiff of urine. Then I saw that the thing the spade had hit was only a large piece of tough clay. I dug away the soil around it, only to find more lumps and stones I could not remember from before. I stood in the impression and heaved them out, wondering with a glancing horror if one of them was a decomposing head. It was the size of a football. I threw it into the brambles and it split in half. It was only clay. I tried again with the spade, a foot deeper, but it would not penetrate the impacted material beneath. The sweat ran down my forehead. I changed my stance and dug at the bottom of the hole, where the legs should be. But the first spadefuls revealed only more stones and bits of fresh broken fern. I looked up and around me. Had I got the wrong place? I went back to where I had begun, prising the damp clods aside, finding the big tree root I had laid across the body. This was where I had been. I made further frantic stabs to my left and right, above me where the head should have been. I climbed out of the hole. My central digging had taken me three feet deep. But there was nothing of Guy, nor any part of him, to be seen.

28

A wood pigeon dashed from the trees behind me, ripping through the leaves. The air felt soft against my neck. I leaned on the spade, my jaw loose. The relief at not having to go through with this was too enticing. I could not trust my discovery.

I paced about the hole, kicking away the foliage at the edges, stabbing with the spade. Ten yards away I found another spot that would have been the only other place big enough for my purpose those few months before. It was too open. There was no fallen tree. I jabbed the ground with the spade. It stopped barely an inch below the surface, on impacted clay that I would never have been able to move. I went back to the original clearing. It was overlaid with familiarity. This was the place. Yet it seemed too certain. I made two forays towards the road side of the wood, despite knowing I had been unable to see the road before. I went back and checked the other way, towards the fields behind the wood. I found another small clearing and tested it with the spade, only to find the same hard ground, unmoved for decades. Back at the first hole I made three more deep incisions. There really was nothing there.

I wanted to believe that the lime had worked, for the joy it would bring. But that would have been a miracle and I did not feel my stock was high enough for such a thing – I had been on a losing streak for too long. The lime could not have been so effective. There would have been some bony traces at least. And I still did not know if I had used the right stuff. I shovelled back the loosest of the soil, a token effort, and picked up the sheet and went back to the car.

Driving home, since there was nowhere else to go, I looked blankly at the countryside. My mind was empty. Nothing would register – my hands on the wheel, the shifting of gears, my checking of the road at a roundabout, were the only clues to my existence. They were the distillation of it. My prepared energy had not been required. I felt incredibly happy.

It was over, of course, but at least now I knew my fate. I wondered about Maisie. Would they have her already? I had failed her, though I had made extraordinary efforts on her behalf. No more running around and no more lies. The relief was massive. Drily, I considered the sentence I might get as an accessory to manslaughter. Five years at most? Three, with what they called good behaviour? And weren't the courts famously lenient with first-time offenders? Or would my bankruptcy put me in a poor light? And what if they decided it was murder? But that could not be. I would defend my niece stoutly. There was the medical evidence. She was a miracle baby, though maybe God had not been so kind and there was the chance she had been damaged at birth. It might be as well for me to think about that, to say I was forearmed with this knowledge when I first thought to cover up the incident. Sir, I did not think she would be believed . . . I chuckled. And why not? I had earned these last few minutes of freedom, now I had the luxury of knowing how it would end.

This mood of bemused resignation persisted as I drove back into Oughton and up to the Finlandia. In the garage, as a last gesture to discretion, I ran the soles of my boots and the blade of the spade under the cold tap, returning them to their place in the corner. I put back the pick, tossed the sheet on a high shelf, locked the car and went outside. The sky was clearing to the sweetest blue. Kids were running happily along the street beyond the garden wall. My eyes prickled. This could have been such a beautiful day. I looked at the sky, hoping for some kind of release, hanging around thinking these last moments alone might be priceless. Then I went inside.

The confines of the kitchen afforded an instant depression. I wanted to go back out into the open, that lovely coastal morning. If I could have got away with this, I would never have left Oughton. Why should I? There was a happiness here that anyone could find, should they choose to look. But it was too late for thinking that now. I was here and in trouble.

Andy was fixing the lunchtime meals and bar snacks, wrapping french bread rolls in his swishy clingfilm. He smiled coolly in a way that once again suggested he knew all about my predicament. 'What about lunch, Harold?'

Was this his idea of a joke? I clasped my hands in thought, playing what I believed was an absurd game. 'Oh, a piece of the veal pie, I think. It looked quite nice.'

'A few sautés?'

'Yes. Why not?' I laughed.

Andy had a knife in his hand, his smile becoming clotted, a sideways skew of the lips, the flaring of a nostril as if he knew he would not have to prepare this meal for me. I would not have time for it. The police were waiting somewhere. His suggestion of lunch was a ploy of their making, to get me where they could pounce. God, how dreary this was going to be! I wanted it over with. Andy returned to making the snacks, counting prawns onto lettuce beds. He had never really liked me, and now he was pleased that I would no longer have any say in the running of the hotel. He would want to be around when they came for me, hopeful of a struggle, a scene I would not make. In a surge of awareness, I found myself standing in the middle of the kitchen thinking these things. I just wanted to be picked up and moved, without fuss, making it easy for whoever was coming for me. I went through to the lobby, smiling facetiously, expecting hands about my person at every second.

All seemed normal. It was a brilliant deception, a tease, Mary breezing across the lobby, Lionel in the bar getting a drink for the first of the new arrivals whose suitcases were standing by the desk. It was so peaceful, it was heartbreaking. Or maybe I had this wrong? How could the police have extracted a body from a woodland grave and left the scene unmarked and unattended? Had that been the trap? Had I been followed all morning? How come I had not thought of this earlier? Was I really so dozy? I felt quite faint, unable to take another transformation of my ideas. This new doubt was more troubling than the prospect of being arrested. Could this please be over soon? Then I looked into the office and saw that it would be.

My appearance at the door halted Mother's conversation. 'Ah,' she said, sitting back, her hand on her gold necklace. 'This is my son. Harold – '

'I know. We've already met.' I extended a hand to my captor. 'Mr Pinney. How are you?'

29

Pinney invited me to sit down – in my own office. Already he was taking responsibility for my existence, making an object of me. These would be my first rites in the calling of a criminal, a murky oblivion I was sobering to, and might even find intriguing. It was the moment of true guilt, easier to face than I had thought, though for its revelation I should have liked Mother's seat, the swivel chair with the fraying cushions. It would have put me face to face with my prosecutor. But I had to make do with pulling up an old bar stool from beside the safe. I sat down between them, awaiting the arrival of undeniable facts.

'Looks like it might turn out fine,' he said, turning over the pages of his notepad.

'Yes,' I said, pleasantly enough.

'Your mother tells me business is quite good.'

'It's been worse, for this time of year.'

'July and August would be your best time, I would guess.'

'You'd guess right.'

This preamble irritated me. I had no need of it. I wanted the whole terrible story out in the open, no hanging around.

Pinney looked at me seriously, like a doctor about to reveal the disturbing results of a blood test. The jaw dropped, working from side to side. Now we would get down to business. 'You'll know why I'm here, of course.'

Beside me, Mother was stroking the lapel of her blouse. She yawned. Another minute and her life would be devastated. I felt a boyish shame and wondered if I should ask for her to leave the room. Or was it better this way, brutal perhaps, but saving me the awful explanation I would have to make later? 'Well,' I said, 'I imagine it's about the missing lad.'

The policeman put his hands on the edge of the desk. 'The thing is, Mr Broome, we've been obliged to look at the case again. I understand Mr Winterton's brother and mother have been down here.'

I looked at Mother. She was fussing with the cuffs of her cardigan, unruffled by this information. 'They stayed here, at the hotel.'

'I know. They told me.' He sat back, crossing his legs, head on one side. 'The problem is, they seem to think you know more about Guy's whereabouts than you've let on.'

'Really?'

He lifted his hands in an open gesture. 'They seem convinced.'

In my mind's eye I saw Adam bawling at him, the mother sobbing at his side, my name written in fire on the air of a police-station office. Pinney's gaze did not flinch from me. It was my turn to answer, but I could not think what to say. A blurting confession would have been untimely, the sequence of the procedure had not yet called for it. And besides, the tension was getting too much for me. I felt tired, a little sick. Would I be handcuffed? Might I have to stay here in Oughton at the local constable's? Would they let me pack a bag?

197

'You see, Harold . . .' The use of my first name was calculated, part of the softening-up routine. 'This puts us in a difficult position.'

'Sorry?'

He sucked at his teeth. 'Put it this way. Cases like this can inspire publicity. I'm sure you noticed yourself that Mr Winterton's brother can be a bit of a handful.' He picked his pen up and dropped it. 'He's a firebrand, it can't be denied.'

'I'd spotted that,' I said with a chuckle.

'Mmm.' He turned in his chair, leaning on his elbow on the desk. Behind his shoulder was a red and blue Les Routiers wall sticker. 'The thing is, despite our misgivings, and certainly the cost to the force, we have to be seen to have exhausted all possibilities.'

'Of course,' I said, wishing he would get to the point.

'So, what we have to do, what we have to be seen to be doing . . .' He leaned further over, a clutter of things about him, the pad and pen, keys, a radio with which I imagined he would summon his helpers. Were they in the bushes outside? Might the building be surrounded? The idea amused me. They should come inside, have a drink in the bar while these tedious formalities were dealt with. He flicked over two pages of the notepad. 'You said you had never seen Guy Winterton?'

'Did I?'

He looked up, mouth open. 'You did say that, Harold.'

My palms were sweaty. I thought of making a move for the scotch in the drawer. It did not seem unreasonable, yet I could not find the nerve to reach for it. I dried my hands on my shirt front. 'Yes. I did say that.'

'But you knew your niece'd had a troubled relationship with someone?'

Now he was trying to put the words in my mouth, to bend the case, perhaps to make it fit some procedural requirement. The things they said about the police were true. They were not averse to abstracting the truth. It put me on the defensive, less ready to play the game. 'I seem to remember saying she probably had a number of admirers.' Pinney nodded. Now it was my turn to lie. Why make it so easy for him? 'She's told me about Guy since.'

'Oh?'

'I know you went to see her.' It was a point I wanted to make about the trouble he had caused her.

He scratched the corner of his mouth. His teeth were yellowed. A decade of police tea and biscuits, I thought. Refreshment in the course of prosecuting for the safety of the public, defending its capricious morals. My restlessness was turning to petulance. I saw myself in court, loud and angry, lambasting the judge, denying everything.

'Was Guy Winterton ever at this hotel?' The tone was more formal. We were getting close to the truth. I might yet make a run for it, a mad afternoon spent dashing about the coast, the geography of which I knew better than he.

'No.' This was a truth. It calmed me, a balance against the lies.

'And you never saw him in the resort?'

'I didn't, no.'

'Why did you give the Wintertons a false name?'

I shifted on the stool, embarrassed for Mother, who was now looking at me with the faintest of smiles. 'I think you said yourself, the fellow looks like trouble. I didn't want him bothering Maisie. She's a young girl, on her own.'

A shaft of sunlight came through the window, warming my thigh through the old jeans I had put on that morning for the express purpose of exhuming a body. A new cloud passed over the sun and the warmth faded instantly. Mother lit a cigarette, offering one to Pinney which he refused, waving the packet away, deep in thought. Outside the office, Lionel was cheerful and noisy, greeting another new guest. Kipper was sniffing at the door. He yapped to be let in. Lionel chivvied him away. Pinney looked at the door. He was searching for the right words to nail me. The silence was unbearable.

'Well,' he said. 'I have to say I don't think there's anything else we can do.' He looked down, his gaze fixed in the mid-distance between him and the desktop, his jaw still. 'You have told me everything you know, haven't you, Harold?'

My heart hit a low thumping rhythm. This would put years on me. How much longer would it be going on? 'I have.'

'There's nothing you want to add? Nothing you've thought of over the last few weeks?'

I said nothing. My guilt had become a simple humiliation, holding my tongue.

'Harold?'

'No.'

He put his hands in his lap. 'Well, that seems to be that, then.'

'Sorry?'

'I don't see there's much point in going on with it. This chap Guy, he wasn't the most predictable of people. And . . .' He paused to check his watch and scribble the time on his pad. 'We've had a sighting.'

I went light-headed. The sun came back to the window, a bar of shifting light, further down my leg. 'What do you mean?'

'He's been seen.' He took off his glasses, revealing watery

green eyes, like a turtle's. 'In Liverpool. Or at least someone thought they'd seen him, or someone like him. They spotted him on a photograph on the station wall. The Liverpool lads checked it out. There was someone hanging around the area who looked very much like Guy, but he'd gone when they got there. And so, I suppose, given the vagueness of it all . . .' He put back the glasses and looked directly at me. 'I'd have to say that's probably good enough.'

'Well,' said Mother. 'If someone's seen him, what's the point in going any further?'

I put my arm across my stomach, nipping my lips as if pondering the case. It was too much to take in. I was cheating him. Or was this an elaborate ploy? I kept the pose, digging my elbow into my wrist, affecting an air of modest concern.

'There isn't much point, to be honest, Mrs Broome. We'd like it sorted out properly, but there's just so little to go on.' He put his pen in his pocket, a gesture that loosened in me a relief both wild and suspect. When he stood, I was on my feet too. A reflex action, too sudden. 'Well, once again, thank you for your time, Harold. And you, Mrs Broome.'

Mother lifted her necklace, blowing on the ruddy skin in the V of her blouse. 'It was nothing. I'm sorry we couldn't be more help.'

Pinney dropped the radio in his shirt pocket. 'Oh, it's just one of those things really. Perhaps they'll find him through the missing-persons bureau. Or the Sally Army. To be honest, they're rather better at it than we are. People can be very reluctant to talk to the police these days.' He grinned. 'No one trusts us much. It's the modern world. What can you do?'

Somewhere behind me, Mother rose to her feet, holding the edge of the desk for support. Pinney offered me his hand

201

and I shook it, the action taking place somewhere below my wildly racing thoughts. 'Goodbye then, Harold.'

'Yes. Cheerio.'

Each of his small movements made me trust him less, but his leaving, with Mother limping gallantly without her stick, showing him round the reception desk and across the lobby to the door, was as genuine as could be. Mother said something that made him laugh loudly. They exchanged goodbyes and he was away, skipping down the steps. I went back into the office, my legs weak. I sat down on the chair he had used. It was still warm. Mother came back and closed the door.

'He seems satisfied,' she said.

'Does he?'

'Yes. He does.'

I closed my eyes. The remnants of my guilt remained. I had been carrying this secret too long. It was almost at the surface, like a burrowing mole. It had to come out. 'Listen, Mother. I think he'll be back. There's something I have to tell you.'

She put her hand on my shoulder. 'There's no need.'

'No, no, you don't understand. Listen to me – '

'Harold, no.' I looked up. She was breathing heavily, a mist of sweat on her rouged cheeks, her lips dry. 'I know all about it.'

'You know all about what?'

'The whole story. About Guy.'

I shook my head. 'There's more to it than you think. You don't understand . . .'

She shifted her hand up to my neck and squeezed, the skin of her fingers hard and cold. 'I do understand.' She raised her eyebrows. That look, the matriarch. I was nine years old again. 'Harold, I know everything.'

202

30

'Maisie told me, the night before she went down to Nottingham. She was in a state. She couldn't face going down there. She hadn't even packed.'

We had moved up to Mother's lounge. She was sitting on the pile of cushions in her armchair, pouring a glass of sherry. It disappeared in three gauged mouthfuls, her hand shaking as she put the glass on the table at her side. 'She wanted to go to the police.' She rubbed her eye with her palm and blew her nose.

I was sitting on the sofa, but I had to stand again. 'What did you say to her?'

There was an air of weariness about her, face pink with the sherry. 'I told her she should trust you, that you were a good man and what you were doing was right. Please sit down, Harold. I can't be doing with you hovering around.'

A glumness came over me, the complex depression of a man who has duped a judge and jury but cannot allow himself the freedom suddenly laid before him. I had been prepared for the worst; but it had not happened. And now the world felt fake. I sat down, covering my eyes, shaking my head. 'I don't know what to say. I'm sorry. You've known all this time.'

'I always knew something was up. That day . . . you were acting so strangely.'

'Was I?'

'And you were seen.' She looked at the decanter beside her, but made no move for it.

My stomach fell. A last ripple of anxiety. I dreaded any talk of bodies or digging. This was my mother. It was the most raw conversation of our lives. Despite my curiosity, the moments thudded by, our mutual company almost intolerable. 'Seen where?'

She looked up, raising her head, stretching the loose skin under her chin. 'Out in the woods. Ben Clancy, from Carnham. We used to buy a few pheasants from him. He hunts, illegally of course. I saw him a few days after that weekend. He said he thought he'd recognised you in the woods, though he hasn't seen you since you were a lad. He didn't know what you were doing there, but he thought you looked agitated. And if anything ever went on up there, he'd remember. People forget nothing round here. And there was someone else.'

'Who?'

'Sheila, my hairdresser. She saw you at the garden centre. I won't ask what you were doing there.'

'You can't move round this bloody place.' I was angry, but it was only to mask my humiliation at being found out. I looked at the ceiling. The carriage clock on the mantelpiece tinkled the half-hour. Kipper stirred from behind the sofa and crossed the rug, slumping at Mother's feet. She had her eyes closed, head dropping as if sleep was seconds away. She was doing her best, but I knew there was more to it than she realised. This was not the reprieve she was hoping to bring me. I leaned forward. 'But the . . .' I could not bring myself to be graphic. 'Where I put him. It's not there any more.'

She opened her eyes. 'I know.'

'What do you mean, you know? How could you know?'

'I had it moved.'

'What?' I shook my head in disbelief. 'You can't have.'

'When I had a proper grasp of what was going on, I got Lionel – '

'Oh, for God's sake, no! Mother – '

'Shush. I got him to keep an eye on the area. You're a resourceful man, Harold. And you're intelligent, even though you've wasted it most of your life.' She was addressing the hearth rug, spilling this last comment for the first time in my life. 'Anyway, I didn't think you'd have the stomach for watching out yourself. And when I heard they were felling the place, I asked him for a favour.'

'But Lionel . . .' I groaned. The glimmering redemption I was beginning to get used to was snatched away. Now there would be no escape from it all, ever. Half the town was involved. There would be rumours, a wordless anticipation given body by whispers round the market, jokes in the pubs, even Colin might already know something. The Finlandia would be a place of secrets, its respect irretrievable. I would have to leave as soon as possible. 'Why Lionel? I mean, how do you know you can trust him?'

'He was in the army. He fought in the Falklands. Goose Green.'

'So?'

'Your father did a great deal for him, taking him on here. You wouldn't know, you weren't around, but Lionel had a cloud hanging over him when he got out of the forces.' She was tracing her bottom lip with the tip of her tongue. 'Some allegation of brutality. I've never known the proper story, I didn't want to. Nothing was ever proved against

205

him. It got covered up, somehow. But this is such a small place. I don't think you've ever appreciated that.'

'I think I have.'

The decanter was irresistible. She poured a small measure, the reach of her hands looking alien, the action of someone I did not really know. 'Lionel's father and yours were great friends, you know. Your dad helped set him up in that tool-hire place he had. They were very loyal to each other, like men can be, if they want. I know you've never seen eye to eye with Lionel, but he's been good to me. It's been a lonely affair since Reg died. And then Matthew went away. You create a family thinking it'll be for ever. But it doesn't work out like that.' She said this coolly, a rebuke for both her wayward sons. She put her hands on the chair arms, the firm set of her mouth making the picture of abandonment complete.

'I hope you didn't pay him.'

'I had to give him something for his trouble.'

'Mother!'

She tutted. 'There was money from Reg's insurance. It was enough to implicate him, that's all. A bit of business.'

I wanted to say more, but nothing would have been right. She was sitting forward, the self-esteem built carefully over her lifetime lying in ruins. I wanted to apologise for my rebuke, to hug her, yet the gesture would have been too calculated. I was the selfish son, the one who could get little right in his life. I went to stand by the window, looking down at the seaside town about its small business, the people coming and going under the red and white striped awning of the baker's shop, not giving a glance to the Finlandia and its momentous concerns. I looked back at Mother. She was staring into the cold fireplace.

'Where did Lionel put the body?' I needed to know. This could not be asked later.

The direct reference to Guy left her unmoved, perhaps even pleased to be dealing with the situation on a matter-of-fact level. 'I don't know. You can ask him, if you like, but he says it's better if he just keeps it to himself. He told me it'll never be found, and I believe him. Like I said, he was a soldier. He'll have known what he was doing. Trust him, Harold.'

'It seems I've no choice.'

'No. You haven't.' She took a tissue from a box by the decanter and dabbed at the corners of her eyes. It was hard to tell whether this was an affectation or she was crying.

I said, 'Maisie's the one who might crack.'

'I know. You'll need to keep an eye on her, keep in touch. We both will.'

My father was watching me from the photograph on the mantelpiece. Beyond him was the painting of Maisie. I turned back to the window. Across the street a man was bawling at his infant daughter, trying to get her to keep up with the rest of the family. The girl, with brown curls and spotty beach dress, folded her arms defiantly, sitting on the pavement, scowling. The father came back and scooped her up, kicking and squealing.

Mother's voice came from across the room. 'The boy was a shit, Harold.'

'What?'

'That Guy. He was a waster, an animal. He raped your niece.'

'That's what Maisie says.'

'It's true! You have to believe her.'

I was still watching the street. The family was making its way through the Rose Gardens. I could hear Mother getting up behind me. 'What about those dizzy spells or whatever it is she has?' I said. 'I didn't know about that.' For once, I was prepared to accept her as an authority on the subject.

'It's nothing. It hasn't happened for ages.' She came up to me, leaning on the stick, eyes wide and angry. 'Maisie's my grandchild. She told you the truth. You believe her, Harold. And you don't trouble yourself about that youth. He was trash. He got what he deserved. Forget him. Get on with your life.' The arm leaning on the stick was quivering, betraying a loathing hoarded up over the many decades of her life, a depth of bitterness I had not realised before. It was a spite known by those she did not like, but forgiven or ignored by the rest of us.

'Well, frankly, what is my life?' I gave a grim snigger. 'It's just one failure after another, the odd catastrophe thrown in for good measure.'

'Don't be stupid. You're feeling sorry for yourself. You've always been like that.'

Spits of rain arrived, tapping on the glass. Down below, a group of lads came by, one of them wearing a novelty hat with a big padded yellow fist on the peak, the ringleader perhaps. The older walkers were producing raincoats, umbrellas, looking at the sky, up towards me, trying to calculate the extent of the downpour. 'Have I?' I said.

EPILOGUE
CHRISTMAS DAY

31

This year, in what was once a tradition, the family takes the Finlandia's dining room for itself. Mother's favourite china gets its annual outing and four tables are pushed together and covered with a gold and ivory Irish linen cloth that belonged to my grandmother. The heating is on full and the main door and the door to the bar are locked. And in the kitchen I am making lunch, with my brother beside me offering ribald suggestions about the turkey. 'Well stuffed, like a Siamese prostitute.'

Matthew came back three days ago. His hair is a dusty fawn, making it difficult to tell which is genuine grey. Inevitably, he looks older than last time I saw him, a little piece of his life recently surrendered, a donation to time. 'Tell you what, I've been looking forward to this.' He pours more wine for us both. 'It's something you miss. And you dream about the cold, good sharp cold. You know, I expected to be wearing thick woollies and vests when I came back. But I just don't feel it yet. Maybe I'm all stored up with vitamin D or whatever it is.'

He wears glasses, as he has for the last five years. His moustache is thick and he has not shaved. My brother is taller and thinner than me. It has always been this way. 'What'll you do when the contract's up? Will you stay?'

'I don't know. There's plenty of work. They're making it into a millionaires' playground for when the oil runs out. It's the same in Saudi. But you get sick of the heat. You put the air conditioning on at night and wake up at four o'clock, freezing fucking cold. And the students can be a pain. Some of them, the fathers are so rich they just don't need to train at anything. They'll get fed up after a month and decide they want to be doctors or bloody airline pilots. And Christ, Harold . . .' He takes a drink and holds up the glass. 'It's so fucking dry out there!'

We both laugh. 'What, no drink at all?'

'Ah, you can get one of these card things.' He makes a half rectangle with his thumb and forefinger. 'So you can brew the stuff yourself. But it's not the same. You can't relax.' He looks around the kitchen, the condensation running on the windows and walls. 'It's still strange without the old man here,' he says, filling his glass again. 'This was his place, really, wasn't it?'

'I know what you mean.'

'Still, you're here now. That surprised me, to be honest. I thought you'd have cleared off again by now.'

I turn the heat down on the carrots and check the potatoes roasting in the big oven. With the mild effects of the drink, I think that I love my brother – these moments are so pleasant I want them to last for ever. Why can't life be like this all the time? 'Yes. I suppose I've surprised myself.'

'Are you staying then, or what?'

'Looks like it. At least for now. I don't know what else I could do, what with the bankruptcy and all that. It'll be a while yet before I'm discharged.'

'Sounds like you're waiting to get out of the bloody army.'

212

'Yes. Thing is, though, I don't feel particularly ambitious any more.'

Matthew nods slowly, chewing over my words. 'She'll be pleased.' He holds up his glass in the direction of the dining room. 'The old lady, she likes having you around.'

'I know.'

'And Maisie. She says you've been good to her. A proper uncle. I owe you, old mate.'

For a brief, dizzying moment, I wonder what he's talking about. I rinse my fingers under the cold tap and take a sip of wine. 'Don't worry about it.' He knows nothing, of course, though I cannot look at him. For all that Matthew is rougher-edged than me, Oughton through and through, in my position he would have played a straight bat and gone to the police. 'Maisie is family. We all are. We have to look out for each other, don't we?'

'You're right there.' He is leaning on the worktop, looking serious. 'Christ, you're right.'

A maudlin mood threatens. 'I'm going to get the trolley. Do you want to tell them it'll be five minutes?'

'Right, captain. Will do.' And he disappears into the dining room and says a few words that are followed by his booming laughter.

The summer was a mixed affair, with rains and hail at the end of August and a ruinous spring tide that swiped away pieces of the cliff beneath the golf course to the south. In October, the sea threw up one of its curiosities, a forty-foot humpbacked whale. It came aground near the Head and I went to look at it, the barnacle-crusted mouth, the slash lines on its underside, its tiny eyes already mushy, tissues deflated. You could smell it from a hundred yards away. I didn't know what I was doing there. For some reason I

213

thought it might be symbolic, but it was as if there was a skin over my perceptions. I was beyond the visibly meaningful, my existence in a state of flux, a virtual reality.

In November I was forty and I did not become morose, nostalgic or changed in any way. I had thought to become one of those insufferable people for whom life, by legend, begins at such an age, though in truth it was an event I barely noticed, save for musing on the idea that in living there is no final gain, there is only renewal, the starting of things. Yet even this was no more than a remote idea, easily accepted. To be neurotic about getting older seemed to me a matter of choice. What would have been the point? Life was a little empty, naturally, though it could have been worse. Tiredness, perhaps, was my only real complaint.

I stayed on at the Finlandia because I did not have the energy to run away. But no one came bothering us, not Pinney, not Adam with his threats or the baseball bat I imagined he had in mind for me. Lionel and I stood side by side during the busy season, working the bar. My debt to him hung heavy in the air, and once I thought he was about to mention it to me, but we were interrupted. And so not a word was exchanged between us about Guy and, in his turn, Lionel was less sarcastic, even respectful. I still did not trust him, and I daydreamed about him finding a job somewhere else, though while he was still here with Mother and me I felt certain he could not be disloyal.

Maisie quit her studies at the end of the summer term. She had her hair cut and now she gels it straight. It makes her look older, which is what she wants, she says. She came back to Oughton and stayed at the house alone while she looked for work. Some days, when she came to see us, she would say she wanted to teach English abroad. At other times it would be voluntary work, or computers. Once she announced to me that she had become a vegetarian, fixing me with a glassy look, daring me to challenge the idea. It was as if she was regressing to some point in her early youth, rejecting the idea of adulthood. Then another time, over a drink in a village pub, she confided that when the year was over she would be able to think more clearly, feel less 'stiff', whatever that meant. She seemed to want to say more, but couldn't. It was the closest she came to mentioning what we had done together and I felt no inclination to bring up the matter myself. The time was passing and the world remained silent on the subject of Guy.

In the New Year I will be divorced, and I think it will make me happy. It could have been over sooner, but Nicola stalled the proceedings. She has been back to, and left again, her letter-writing lover. In one anguished half-minute phone call she said she still loved me. And then she hung up.

The winter is not yet cold. Like Matthew, I am hoping for snow, of course, and that icy wind that cleanses the air and brings blood to the cheeks.

After lunch I drive us all down to the seafront and sit on a bench with Mother while Matthew and Maisie take Kipper on the sands. The sea is dark and swelling, the sky ribboned with grey and winter gold. 'They say it's nearly fished out,' says Mother, staring at the sea. 'What'll everyone do then?'

'They'll stick to meat, I imagine.'

She laughs, her chin down in her scarf to hide it from the breeze. 'It's so nice having us all together.'

'Yes, I know.'

'Look at Matthew. Look at him!'

My brother had been throwing a piece of kelp for the dog to chase, and now Kipper is stranded on a sandbank with the tide rolling in around him. Matthew runs through the water to bring him back to safety. Mother laughs. 'He'll be soaked.'

When the dog is back on the sands, Maisie calls to him and they run together along the line of the tide. She is too fast for him and he drops to the sand, panting, watching her. But Maisie keeps running. Then she stops suddenly, looking out to sea, motionless, the wind wrapping her long black skirt round her legs.

'Is there something wrong with her?' asks Mother.

'No, I don't think so.'

'I thought she . . .'

'You thought she what?'

'No. It's all right. It's nothing.'

Matthew chases after Maisie, Kipper recovered and trotting behind him.

To the north of the bay children and couples in bright coats are clambering on rocks of the Head, the livid sea swiping at the rocks, looking for victims among those who stray too far, ignorant of the tide. On the Head itself, the grass is a dull green suede, a cap above the exposed red clay. Each year there is less and less of it, the sea clattering at the bottom, the rain turning the top and sides to mud. But there is enough to fascinate the visitors yet, to draw them, even on this day, as it does in summer, as it has since time first lifted it from the sea.

When Matthew gets to Maisie he puts his arm around her and she lets her head rest on his shoulder. Mother is watching them, their slow walk back in the fading light.

In the evening we are back at the hotel in Mother's lounge, watching television. Matthew sleeps, but Mother forces herself to stay awake, as if frightened of missing a second of our company. She makes herself eat the mince pies and the shop-bought yule log and admires again the pretty embroidered jumper Matthew brought her from Kuwait. Maisie lolls on the floor, gorging on chocolates and watching a film, her attention taken by it completely.

Later, Matthew and Maisie go home and Mother succumbs to sleep. I cover her with her tartan blanket, turn the fire down and go to bed. For all the day's indulgences, I do not feel particularly tired. But sleep will come soon. And I'm hoping it will be an untroubled night, free of those occasional dreams in which I see a patch of skin showing in the earth, a knee, a dirty closed eye. On those nights I wake in a sweat, knowing that what I did was wrong. And more than once I have cried out, but if Mother hears me she does not mention it. Then I sleep again, deep and dreamless, a reliable pattern.

Until the next time.

A NOTE ON THE AUTHOR

Paul Sayer's first novel, *The Comforts of Madness*, won the 1988 Whitbread Book of the Year Award. He is also the author of *Howling at the Moon*, *The Absolution Game* and *The Storm-Bringer*.